THE SEEING EYE

Celebrated art critic Oswald Burke, who had upset many with his strong opinions, is found murdered in London's Westminster Art Gallery. The obvious suspect is an old lag, who is there for the purposes of robbing the safe. But David Wintringham and his wife Jill turn part-time detectives and soon find themselves embarrassed by a plethora of suspects, including two young artists, whose work plays a part in the solution of the mystery.

THE SEEING EYE

Josephine Bell

First published 1958
by
Hodder & Stoughton Ltd

This edition 2007 by BBC Audiobooks Ltd
published by arrangement with
the author's estate

ISBN 978 1 405 68577 1

British Library Cataloguing in Publication Data available

Printed and bound in Great Britain by
Antony Rowe Ltd., Chippenham, Wiltshire

Chapter I

THE Wintringhams climbed the wide steps of the Westminster Art Gallery, pausing frequently to look back at the river, revealed as they mounted.

It was a wild spring day, with a wind from the south-west that tore at them in warm gusts from between the sheltering buildings; that bent horizontal the spindly twigs of the plane trees; that poured unhampered eastwards along the broad sweep of the Thames, driving spray-flecked waves before it. A watery sun shone as best it could from the ragged gaps in the clouds. On the roadway the dust swirled, and the litter rustled; discarded newspapers wrapped themselves about the railings below the steps; the gutters were filled with squashed cartons and muddy wrappings.

"I shall lose my hat," Jill cried against the wind, laughing as she held it down with her free hand. But her words were carried away in a thunderous gust, and David did not hear them. She ran up the rest of the steps to find shelter, and after a moment, dragging his eyes from the lively slapping progress of a tug with barges coming up-river from Westminster, David followed her. They pushed through the turning doors and found themselves in the still, sedate quiet of the pillared hall.

Jill took a mirror from her handbag and looked at herself in it. The short climb from the street to the door; the few minutes from sheltered car to peaceful interior had, in that wind, wrought dire havoc to her appearance.

"I'll have to go and tidy up," she said, making ineffectual efforts to rearrange her hair with one gloved hand.

David looked at her glowing cheeks and amused eyes.

"You look charming," he said. "But just as you like. I have the whole afternoon free, thank God."

5

"Charming for the country walk, perhaps," Jill answered. "I won't be a minute. I should hate to let you down. We might meet one of your eminent patients, or distinguished colleagues."

"Most unlikely. I'm sure they are all worse Philistines than we are. I'll meet you inside."

"Stay near the door, then."

Jill hurried away. David moved off, following the arrows marked on white cards, and presently found himself moving into the room that housed the current exhibition of Contemporary Art.

There were pictures hanging on the walls, and mobiles hanging from the ceiling. There were sculptures set on stands, and, near the door, where David waited, there was a collection of small tables, surmounted by trays, upon which were set out collections of objects, carefully arranged according to the wayward dictation of the subconscious.

David looked in his catalogue, and looked again at these exhibits in the light of what he had read. The symbols became no easier to understand, the patterns meant just as little. The trays still seemed to him to hold a jumbled collection of commonplace articles. He was reminded of a party game of his youth, in which a very similar tray was exposed for thirty seconds to the eager gaze of the guests, after which they were expected to write down the names of the twenty or so objects they had seen. He had been good at this game, and had often won it, since he had been born with an observing eye and an excellent memory. He amused himself now, while he waited for Jill, by playing the old game with himself. He looked at an exhibit with great concentration for thirty seconds, and then, turning his back on it, and taking out his diary, wrote down the things he had seen. Turning back to check his answer, he found a couple of well-dressed women staring at him with mingled awe and curiosity. Quite plainly they had been impressed both by his concentrated attention and subsequent notes. As he caught their eyes they turned away, and he heard Jill's voice beside him.

"Where do we start?"

"I've started already."

He told her how he had been amusing himself, and of the effect it had had upon the two women.

"I expect they thought you were a top-ranking critic, summing up the exhibit and making notes for your future article."

"I do hope they did. Do you mind waiting while I check up my answer?"

"Baby!"

Jill looked at a few of the other tables, but found nothing inspiring there, and came back.

"Two missed out, and three described wrong," said David. "Interesting mistakes from a psychologist's point of view, but I won't bore you with them."

"What's the thing meant to be, anyhow?"

They looked for the number of the exhibit, and found none. So the catalogue could not help them.

"What do you think has happened to the number?"

"Come unstuck and got brushed away? Snatched off by an irate or bemused viewer? Perhaps it never had one."

"Oh," said Jill, enthusiastically. "Do you think it's been put together by the visitors? An expression of the *collective* subconscious?"

"That's a delightful idea! Let's add our quota."

David searched his pockets, discarding this and that grubby, unrecognizable piece of rubbish. At last he brought out a small paper packet of cardboard matches.

"Swiss ones, too," he said, proudly. "Still intact, and it's two months since we were at Arosa."

He placed the matches carefully among the other objects on the tray. No one seemed to notice: certainly no one interfered. Jill, entering into the spirit of the game, fished up two aspirins from the bottom of her handbag and put them near the matches. Still no one protested, no one stopped to ask them what they were doing or why. The crowd of neatly dressed middle-aged people, the scattering of eccentrics, the intermittent stream of untidy arty young, moving in groups, continued to go past, staring, respectful, dumb.

"Pity," said David. "No reaction."

Behind him a man laughed. It was a good laugh. Genuine unself-conscious amusement. Both Jill and David turned round.

A young man was standing close behind them. He wore baggy-kneed corduroy trousers, a check shirt and a duffle coat. His fair hair was very long, but it showed some evidence of combing, and looked reasonably clean. He had a square face and a wide mouth, open just now as he laughed.

"Well," said Jill, "it's nice to be appreciated."

"I'd never have had the nerve," said the young man. He had a pleasant voice, and spoke with the indeterminate accent, one quarter local dialect, and three-quarters B.B.C., now universal in the student world.

"It doesn't take much courage," said David. "Observation among the general public is very low, and expectation of the unexpected even lower. A penalty of urban existence."

"I don't know about that," said the young man. "But I do know they swarm into these shows, which makes it look as if this stuff was highly thought of."

He spoke with a deep bitterness that made the Wintringhams feel uncomfortable.

"Come over here," he continued. He set off towards the nearest corner of the room, seeming to take it for granted they would follow him. Exchanging glances of amused surprise, David and Jill hurried after him.

"What do you think of that?" he asked, as they joined him.

A narrow glass case stood on a table against the wall. In it was placed a row of very old sponges, cut with a pair of scissors into rough, primitive human heads.

"What do you think of that?" the young man repeated.

"It's a nonsense," said David.

"I thought you'd agree. The whole exhibition is a nonsense."

"No," said Jill. "We haven't been round yet, but I'm sure some of the pictures will have something. There are three Picassos, anyway."

"You admire Picasso?"

"Enormously."

"But he isn't modern. His stuff is fifty years old, at least."

"He is still alive, very much so, and still working."

The young man nodded, grudgingly.

"He's about the only one that can draw," he said.

Jill did not attempt to answer this sweeping statement.

The conversation lapsed. David and Jill moved on, concentrating upon the paintings that were the real reason for their visit. The young man dropped behind, but as they moved into the next room, they found him near them again. He smiled at Jill and she smiled back. He drew level with her, and, as David moved ahead, said to her in a low voice, "I thought at first he was the art critic. When I saw him making notes. It wasn't till he put down the matches I knew he couldn't be."

"Which art critic?"

"Oswald Burke."

He spoke the name with the extreme bitterness he had used before, and Jill opened her eyes wide at him.

"Oh! Do you feel like that about him? Of course he does admire this sort of thing. Perhaps he's right. Not about those sponges, if he likes *them*. But he *knows* about pictures, doesn't he? I don't. So I can't really have an opinion about him, except that he writes very well. I suppose I really just like to see what's being done. And sometimes there's a picture that attracts me, or is fully intelligible, or both."

She did not want to be drawn into an argument about art, knowing she was ill-equipped to sustain it. So she moved on more quickly to rejoin David, and the young man was left behind again, and stayed there.

After an hour the Wintringhams felt they had seen enough. As David put it, "The subconscious is so depressingly uniform."

"Do you mean repetitive?"

"Yes. That too."

"They must copy one another consciously, as well. Painters always seem to form groups."

"Modern groups are so much alike."

"Let's go and look at some *real* pictures."

"Hush!"

They wandered away to another part of the Gallery, and then, feeling happier, went downstairs to find tea.

"We expect too much from the contemporary stuff," said Jill. "It's always the same. We expect to find them all works of genius, and so we can't give the second-rate their due. It takes a lot of sifting to find the two or three top painters of a generation. We always expect too much."

"Like our young friend."

"Oh, he was sure it was all complete tripe. But perhaps that was just resentment because he couldn't see anything in it at all."

"He ought to have. At least he seemed to be in the same racket himself. Or a branch of it."

"What do you mean?"

"Didn't you notice the sketch book he was holding? And a pencil, at the ready? He was performing with it, as we were leaving that room. I think he was drawing you."

"I hope not!"

"Why not? An attractive subject."

"Oh, darling! You are an old flatterer. After all these years."

"Don't pretend you don't like it."

They went upstairs again half an hour later, and in the main hall Jill said, "I wonder if our exhibit is still there?"

"Our additions, do you mean?"

"If you like. But I think of it as our exhibit, because I think my aspirins really 'made' it."

"We'll go and see."

The crowd in the exhibition rooms had thinned. Those who stood there now were spending longer over their scrutiny; they stood for minutes at a time, staring from blank faces. All except two men, talking and laughing in the centre of the room, their backs turned to the walls. And the young man in the duffle coat, standing apart, briskly engaged with his sketch book.

"What did I tell you?" said David, nudging Jill as she leaned over the surrealist tray.

"They're still here," she said, in a pleased voice. "And there's another packet of matches, too."

"Perhaps the lad with the pencil provided it?"

"Who? Oh, yes, I see. He looks very absorbed in his work, doesn't he? Is he drawing James, do you think?"

"I wonder. Let's go and ask him."

They moved towards the young man, but as they did so, the two in the centre of the room also moved, and one of them, seeing the Wintringhams, smiled and went towards them.

"Intercepted," murmured Jill, and the next moment she was shaking hands with James Symington-Cole, ophthalmic surgeon at St. Edmund's Hospital. This done, his companion was introduced. Jill found herself greeting Oswald Burke himself.

She was pleasantly surprised by his appearance, and reflected, not for the first time, that a writer's appearance never bore out in any respect the impression made by his writing. Burke, in print, was usually forthright, severe, sarcastic, and at the same time earnest, dedicated, even passionate. The face before her was mild and commonplace, though the eyes that regarded her, politely attentive, were keen. She did not dare to discuss the exhibition with him, but she longed to show him how she and David had taken part in it. Her courage failed her, however, and with a few general remarks, chiefly about the new popularity of art galleries, the conversation came to an end. Burke and Symington-Cole left the room together.

"Now let us see what that boy is doing," said Jill.

He was quite pleased to show them his work. David took the sketch book from him, gave a little gasp of surprise and pleasure, and turned back the pages.

"There you are," he said to Jill. "I told you there was
one of you."

"Oh!"

Jill gazed at the drawing; it was done with great precision,
great economy and grace. In the fewest possible lines she
saw herself, not as the mirror presented her, but recognizably
as something a great deal more.

"Oh," she said again, feeling strangely disturbed.

She handed the book back to David. He did not look at
her, but continued to turn the pages, stopping now near the
end of the series.

"This is brilliant," he said, quietly.

Jill looked again. James Symington-Cole stared at her
from the page. His thin intelligent face was filled with a
kind of avid eagerness, not exactly greed, but akin to it. A
seeking, thirsting, look. The whole expression was tense, and
conveyed a steely ruthlessness she had never before found in
the eye surgeon, but now fully recognized. With a little
shudder she put out a hand and turned the page of the book.
The art critic's very ordinary features, set in a conventional
smile, were conveyed in three or four superbly placed lines.
As a representation of a distinguished important personage
it was almost caricature, perhaps a little cruel.

"You know who this is?" she said, taking the book from
David, and turning it round towards the young man.

"No. I did it when you were talking to him."

"It's Mr. Oswald Burke."

"*That* chap!"

His astonishment was genuine and extreme. He flapped
the pages of the book.

"It could be," he said. "He had a very different expression when he was looking at that frightful stuff over there."

The boy pointed at a structure in fine wire poised on a
short, straight peg. His face wore a curious expression at
that moment, of defiance and some disgust, and also of a
deep, heavy anger. But the look passed, and broke up in a
wholly natural, youthful grin.

"Caught out," he said. "For over a year I've hated that

man's guts. And here he is, nothing to write home about at
all. When I did that one I thought he was some silly bum
who thought he ought to keep up to date."

"What's your name?" asked David, ignoring these
confidences.

"Tom Drummond." He looked from one to the other of
the Wintringhams, and asked, with deliberate casualness,
"What's yours?"

David told him, and went on, in spite of the other's growing hostility, "Are you a professional or do you do this for
fun?"

"Both. Or neither."

"Art school?"

"Should one say, quite obviously?"

"You needn't say anything if you don't want to."

Tom Drummond flushed. David stood, quietly unmoved,
compelling. Jill went to the boy's rescue.

"My husband is on the staff of a teaching hospital. You
mustn't mind him. He spends his life bullying students."

"Look," said David. "You draw like an angel—I think
that is the right expression. No doubt you are aware of it by
now. I want that sketch of my wife, and I'm prepared to
buy it from you for twelve guineas. That is what I think it
is worth now, though as you are unknown, probably, except
to your own group, you would not get as much from anyone
else. In ten years' time I think it will be worth thirty, but I
don't offer more than twelve now. I am quite sure I could
get you the same from Symington-Cole, if you want it. He'd
jump at it."

Tom said nothing. He looked away across the room, and
the Wintringhams, following his gaze, saw it was directed
to a couple who stood before a large canvas on the opposite
wall.

"I'd like to speak to my friends," said Tom, at last. "I'll
be back in a minute."

They watched him go. The attendant at the door got up
and walked into the second room of the exhibition.
Evidently he felt it was time the people began to leave,

though he had no power yet to turn them out. Tom checked as the attendant crossed his path, then moved on. His friends turned as he reached them.

One of them was about the same age as Tom, anything in the twenties, but short and frail-looking, with a weak straggly black beard round his chin, and a slightly more robust black growth on his head.

"That one looks pretty revolting," murmured Jill.

"The other doesn't look the same breed at all," said David.

This other was an older man, neatly and well dressed, with carefully brushed iron-grey hair. He had an overcoat hanging from one arm, and a black felt hat in his hand.

"Well, not the Bohemian kind of artist, anyway," Jill agreed.

Tom began to speak to them eagerly, and they nodded staring past him at the Wintringhams, who turned away, beginning to move towards the door. They had no wish to be drawn into further introductions. Already David began to regret his impulse.

They left the gallery and moved across the hall towards the door. But before they reached it Tom Drummond caught them up.

"I think I'd like to let you have the drawings," he said. "But I want to think it over."

"Why not?"

"Where can I find you if I decide to sell them?"

David began to search in his pocket. Jill opened her handbag and got out her card case.

"Here you are," she said.

Tom held the visiting card by one corner and looked at it curiously.

"Archaic, isn't it?" she said, with a laugh. "But I've still got some of the original batch, and they do occasionally come in useful, as now."

Quite clearly the boy had no idea what she was talking about, Jill thought. Prehistoric, those far-off years when one still paid the occasional call, leaving a card, more as a joke than anything else, unless it was some elderly friend of one's parents, who expected it.

"This is your address?" Tom said, turning the card over and back again. Business cards he knew, but this was different.

"That is our address. We've always been there. Belsize Park is the nearest tube station. We're near the Heath. Do you know Keats's house?"

"No."

"Pity, because we're quite close to it. But it's easy to find."

"I'm back most evenings between six and seven," said David. "Come then and have a drink, if you decide to come."

"Thank you, sir."

The 'sir' had evidently slipped out by mistake, for Tom flushed deeply, bit his lip, and turned away with an abrupt gesture and no leave-taking.

David, being used to this form of address from any youth he spoke to, began to walk away. Tom's abrupt departure was uncouth, but many of his medical students were the same. It was extraordinary how they settled down into normally civilized doctors later on.

Jill caught him up at the revolving doors.

"He's rather a pet," she said, as they came out on to the steps into the blue dusk. The wind had died, the river ran in a dark ribbon at the bottom of the ebb, reflecting the lights on its banks.

"Rather an untrained pet, I imagine," said David. "With a streak of the savage in him. I wonder what Burke has done to call up so much downright hate."

"Oh, I don't think he really hates him. It's the artistic temperament. Anyway, I'll find out when he comes to see us."

"If he comes."

"He'll come all right," said Jill, confidently, as they walked down the steps to their car.

Chapter II

THE Wintringhams' house in Hampstead, together with all those in its immediate neighbourhood, had been fortunate enough to survive, not only the war, but the inroads of subsequent development. While many changes were taking place in Haverstock Hill, and its continuation, Rosslyn Hill; while uncounted Victorian semi-mansions on the west side were pulled down or converted into flats, the smaller and very charming balconied houses, leading towards the Heath, were unchanged, and latterly even revived and improved by fresh paint and other signs of appreciative care. The Wintringhams' house, a three-storey one, standing higher than its neighbours on either side, was painted a very pale grey, with a light blue door and window frames. It had been done up the year before, and still looked surprisingly fresh and clean.

The morning after their visit to the Westminster Gallery, Jill stood on the front steps of this house as she had done on so many days for so many years, listening to her husband's parting reminder before he went off to the hospital.

"If a Dr. Thurlow rings up here, tell him to try the Medical School about two this afternoon. I want to have a word with him, personally."

"Thurlow," said Jill, storing the name in her memory. "Anyone else going to try here?"

"I hope not. Unless that young chap we met yesterday decides to make a date. But you can deal with it if he does."

"You mean Tom Drummond?"

"Was that the name?"

"Yes. I don't think he'll bother, though. He didn't look as if it mattered all that much to him. I mean, not as if twelve guineas would save him from starvation."

"Twelve guineas would save anyone from starvation, temporarily, even at present prices."

16

"You know perfectly well what I mean. He didn't look as if he were down to his last penny."

"Twelve guineas means quite something in the way of paint and brushes, too."

"We don't know if he does. We only know he can draw."

"Pencils and paper, then, if you must quibble."

"I don't think he'll come."

"You did, yesterday. I was unsure, then. Bet you a shilling he turns up. This evening."

"Done."

David kissed his wife and swung off down the steps and away to the mews where he kept his car. Jill went back into the house. She wished she could feel more confident that for once she would win a bet with her husband. It would do him good just occasionally to lose, and the young man, Tom, had looked really angry when he left them in the hall at the Gallery the day before. Only then, as David had reminded her, it was she who had expected to see him again. And secretly, she had not altered this opinion. Probably David knew that. It was just like him to pin her down to an opinion professed insincerely.

The morning passed quietly. Jill was lucky enough to have one retainer left from the days of pre-war domestic comfort. Her children's Nanny had stayed on, invaluable and staunch during the war years, stubbornly faithful afterwards, though the promised maids did not reappear. The children grew up and went away to school, even little Peter, who was now in his last year at his prep school. With Nanny, officially retired, but very actively helping in the housework, and a daily who came each morning, Jill managed easily in term time. The holidays were more lively, but Susan, down from Cambridge, where she was working for a history degree, managed to organize her younger sister and brother sufficiently to prevent chaos, and the older boy, Nicholas, a medical student, wisely avoiding his father's hospital, was living in the hostel of his South London hospital school.

The Dr. Thurlow David had mentioned duly rang up and

B

was directed on to St. Edmund's. After she had taken this expected call Jill went out to do her shopping. She was home for lunch. No one else had telephoned, Nanny told her. She allowed herself to feel mildly triumphant.

In the afternoon she worked in the garden at the back of the house. It was only a narrow strip, but reasonably long. In the war they had dug up half of it to grow vegetables, but the patriotic gesture had been very unrewarding, and as soon as possible afterwards they had restored the rose beds and the grass and re-planted the bottom of the garden with flowering shrubs that needed very little attention.

Jill went in to her tea at half-past four with a face glowing from the chill March wind, hands scratched, in spite of gloves, from pruning the roses, and a feeling of smug satisfaction. Tom Drummond rang the bell at exactly six o'clock.

Nanny went to the door, but Jill heard the remembered voice in the hall, and knew that she had lost her bet. In a spirit of mild revenge she stayed where she was. He could have had the politeness to ring up and ask if he could come. The invitation had been very casual. No particular day had been mentioned. Very well, then, she would meet him with altogether old-fashioned formality. Do him good.

Nanny played up magnificently. As she told Jill afterwards, "I thought he needed taking down a peg or two." Having established that he was invited to call, she asked for his name, opened the drawing-room door and announced in a very fair imitation of a starched parlour-maid, "Mr. Drummond, madam."

Tom stepped forward uncertainly, hearing the door close softly behind him. He found himself in very unfamiliar surroundings.

All the way up the hill from Belsize Park Tube station, he had seen the usual mixed façade of the new London; neat, desperately dull shops and houses or blocks of flats, in place of those knocked down by bombs or post-war planners; in between, the hideous over-decorated efforts of the late nineteenth century. And then he had turned down the Wintringhams' road and found himself in another world, another

century: graceful proportions and wide windows, suggesting
an ease of living altogether remote. He had stifled his first
spontaneous visual pleasure in anger. The houses were not
large, nor in any way ostentatious; in fact many of them
were as small as the suburban box in which he had spent
his childhood. But for the most part they were expensively
maintained. One or two might have a neglected air, with
peeling stucco and faded, cracked paint. This only marked
more vividly the discreet well-chosen gaiety of the rest.

He drove his anger, as he had done all that day, to conceal
the fear in his mind. Money, he thought, savagely. You
can do anything with money. The very fact that these houses
did not flaunt it made them more culpable, for they seemed
to take wealth for granted. He could understand the lucky
chap or the hard worker making a bit of a splash when he'd
brought it off. Here he was, faced by established affluence,
he told himself. This was what the modern world was out
to destroy. He was infuriated by his inward æsthetic dismay
at the bare thought of its passing.

By the time he reached the Wintringhams' house Tom had
worked his imagination up to boiling point. These people
must be plutocrats of the worst type. Inside their house
would be all the luxury they were deliberately concealing.
He would almost certainly be ushered in by a butler. All
right. So what?

When, in fact, the door was opened by Nanny, in her plain
grey wool dress and black cardigan, Tom thought, for a wild
moment, that he had come to a guest house, and was con-
fronting the landlady. Having corrected this impression, he
realized the foolishness of all his previous assumptions.
This did nothing to calm his temper, and accounted for the
truculence that Nanny found so distasteful. His entry into
the drawing-room completed his discomfiture, for there was
nothing there, absolutely nothing, to feed his wrath.

He saw a long room of graceful proportions, with windows
at each end and a fireplace in the same wall as the door.
The room was lighted by two reading lamps, and in the soft
light the well-polished furniture glowed darkly. A bright

wood fire flickered on comfortable armchairs drawn up near
it. A large white jug of daffodils stood on a round table
near one window; there were primroses and violets on the
mantelpiece.

Jill Wintringham moved towards the door to shake hands
with him. He looked very young and very bewildered, she
thought. Nanny must have given him a slight shock. The
old woman's antagonism had been very marked.

"How nice of you to come!" Jill said. "Won't you take
off your coat? My husband isn't back yet, but he ought not
to be long."

Tom began to pull off his duffle, and Jill saw, with
approval, that he had taken the trouble to put on a suit for
his visit.

"Stick it in the hall," she said, opening the door again.
"I'll organize some drinks. What do you like? Sherry?
Gin?"

She was gone before he could answer, and he heard her
walking away down the hall. So he followed with his duffle,
and having dropped it on a chair, wandered back into the
drawing-room and began to look at some miniatures hanging on the wall at the side of the fireplace. There were
four, two on each side, of men and women in Regency
clothes.

Jill came in with a tray of bottles and glasses. She put
it down, shut the door of the room, and went over to join
Tom, still gazing at the miniatures.

"Are these copies, or are they genuine antiques?" he
asked. "Do you collect them?"

Jill laughed.

"They are some of my great-great-grandparents, and their
children," she said.

Tom flushed.

"I don't know who did them," Jill hastened to explain.
"Probably nobody very special, or the record would have
been handed down."

"Are they originals or done from portraits?"

"I don't know that, either. But I should think originals.

My mother gave them to me. There were some portraits as well. Her brother had them, as he was the head of the family. My cousin has them now. But they were not quite like these."

Tom wanted to ask who these people were who thought so much of themselves they had their portraits painted several times over, but he curbed his curiosity. Who the hell cared about ancestors now? he asked himself savagely.

Jill settled her visitor in an armchair with a glass of sherry and led the conversation away from her own family history to his. She learned that he had been brought up in a provincial town in East Anglia and that his father was in business.

"He does a bit of painting now and then, himself," Tom explained. "Water colour sketching in the summer. Conventional, old-fashioned stuff, but he has quite an eye for colour. It was a help, that, when I said I wanted to go in for art."

"It would be."

"They'd told him at school they were putting me in for one of these State scholarships, but that wouldn't have helped, only he knew what I could do, because he'd taken me out with him sketching as a nipper, and he felt responsible."

Jill laughed, and Tom joined in. He had lost some of his shyness, and was recovering from the shock of finding his misconceptions proved both false and ridiculous. He sat back in the comfortable armchair, sipping his sherry and wondering why it was so easy to talk to Mrs. Wintringham, whom he did not know at all, and so difficult to get on with Mrs. Felton, the mother of his friend Christopher, whom he had known for several years.

"What exactly does—Dr. Wintringham—do? It is Dr., isn't it?"

"Yes, it is. He is head of the clinical research department at St. Edmund's Hospital. He organizes the research done, and he does some himself. He gives lectures on medicine to the students and he takes them round on his visits to his own cases. He used to take out-patient sessions, but he has given that up now."

"He sounds a pretty important bloke," said Tom, as casually as possible.

"He is one of the senior consultants at the hospital. *I* think he is very important, naturally." And Jill smiled at Tom so frankly that he found himself smiling back, and wishing he had pencil and paper at hand to record her charming devotion.

David came home at half-past six.

"I thought it was you," he said, as he walked into the drawing-room.

"The duffle?" Tom asked.

"Certainly not. There are thousands exactly like it."

"Coming here?" asked Tom, rather nettled at being placed among thousands.

"Yes. Why not? Half my students wear them habitually. I've got one myself. No. It was the sketch book that had fallen on the floor. Won't you bring it in and let us have another look at it?"

Though he still felt a vague resentment, Tom fetched his drawings from the hall and handed them over to David. Patronage was bitter, but he had to acknowledge that neither of the Wintringhams had a patronizing manner. And he needed money more desperately than anyone would have guessed.

David flapped the pages of the book.

"I couldn't get hold of Symington-Cole to-day," he said. "He has gone to some conference or other. But I spoke to his wife on the 'phone and she was rather thrilled. I'd like to show him your work. What about it?"

For answer Tom took back the book and tore out the page.

"Here you are," he said. "Sell it to him if he wants to buy. But I'm not offering you any commission."

He said this with deliberate rudeness, but David did not seem to have heard. He was still turning the pages of the sketch book.

" Where's the one of Burke? " he asked. " You did draw him, didn't you? "

Tom's face changed. The boyish resentment and suspicion vanished, to be replaced by a hard blankness. He suddenly looked much older.

" I tore it up," he said, slowly.

" *You* tore it up! "

The exclamation came from Jill, and Tom turned his head slowly to look at her, but did not answer.

" I don't believe for a moment that you tore it up," she went on. " Why on earth should you? "

He turned away from her, then, whipping round again, held out his hand to David.

" Give it me back," he said, in a voice thick with anger or fear or both. " I didn't come here to be catechized. I'm off."

David moved away from him, still holding the sketch book.

" Don't be silly," he said, calmly. " Have another drink. What was it—sherry—gin? "

Tom looked helplessly from one to the other. He was furious, but he had the sense to see that their attitude was impregnable. Their quiet impersonal goodwill and good temper maddened, while at the same time it disarmed him. Thoroughly bewildered, he took the glass that David held out to him.

" I don't know how old you are," said David, carefully, " or how long you have been at this game. All that matters to me is that you can draw, and that it is obviously a very considerable gift. If you want to use it to make a living, you must adopt a more professional attitude to your work. Don't you think so? "

" I don't see what right you have to lecture me."

" None whatever." David grinned at him, and Tom found himself, much against his will, smiling back.

" Now," said David. " If it won't send you up in the air again, what is the matter with Oswald Burke? "

Again the shutter dropped, communication was extinguished. But after a long silence, Tom said, quietly, "Do you ever read his books?"

"I have read some articles," said Jill.

"All cracking up this abstract stuff." The words came tumbling now. "If you sit down and splash some paint about and let your rotten subconscious find a few crude shapes, symbolic, of course, floating around in it, that's a picture. That's art. Art my Aunt Fanny!"

"There's a lot more to it than that," said Jill. "But what does it matter to you? You can draw, so you start with an advantage. I can't see any harm in being representational if you want to be. Or if you *have* to be. That's what it comes to, isn't it?"

"Yes."

"Then why mind what Mr. Burke says? He's only trying to explain the experimental work of the people who are trying to express themselves in new ways."

"Who cares about their sickening little selves?"

David laughed.

"Only a minority, I'm afraid. But that isn't the point, here. The point is that you have a gift, a real gift, not only a vague wish to be what is called an artist. You can develop it purely commercially, in advertising, posters, and so on——"

"Which is the only line my Dad sees for me," Tom interrupted, bitterly.

"Quite. Or you can go on learning and discovering what you really want to do with it. In which case you need to know and understand what the other chaps are thinking and doing. Burke is a most distinguished exponent of their ideas. So why worry? Why do you hate him so much?"

Tom turned his head away, to look at Jill. He seemed to be considering if she would be more receptive than David to anything he might say: it was a sly look, rather repulsive, she thought.

"Do you remember that friend of mine who was at the exhibition yesterday?"

"The young man with the beard, or the older one?"

"Both, really. The young man with the beard, as you call him, is Christopher Felton. I share a studio with him."

"And the other?" asked David.

"Hugh Lampton. A psychiatrist. Chris is mad keen on him: thinks he's doing wonders for him. I think he's sending Chris round the bend. And this Burke is behind it all."

"What *do* you mean?"

"Because Chris keeps trying to pull off that sort of stuff, and he can't. He went to Lampton to find out if there was anything the matter with his subconscious to stop him painting abstracts. I ask you!"

"He can't be very sure of himself."

"He'll never be sure of anything. Not Chris. You should meet his mother."

"Oh, dear," said Jill. "It's like that, is it?"

"It's unbelievable! Anyway, after he'd been going to Lampton for a couple of months, Chris took it into his head to ask Burke's opinion of his canvases. Pretty good cheek. I wouldn't have had the nerve, myself."

"Well?"

"Well, of course he got the bird. It shook him, but he persists in thinking Lampton will release his genius for him in time."

"You don't agree?"

"There isn't any genius to release." Tom looked from one to the other, and his face flushed. "Chris is my friend, but that doesn't blind me to the fact that he just hasn't got it. Right deep down he knows it, too."

Jill frowned.

"I don't see why you should hate Mr. Burke, simply because he told your friend the truth. Isn't there more to it than that? Did you, by any chance, show him some of your own work?"

Tom's face was transfigured with rage. Then his anger burst from him in tumbled speech.

"I told you I hadn't the nerve. But he saw some things I'd done. At the School. He's a buddy of the Director. He

had me sent up to him. D'you know what he said? In front
of the lot of them? Staring at me with those eyes of his—
like a bloody gimlet! See right into you!—He said, 'You
could do things really worth while if you had the slightest
conception of what art is about. You are like an apprentice
builder who has a natural gift for laying bricks, but no idea
at all what a building is, or what it means.' Who told him
my father is a builder, and my grandfather was a bricklayer?
Why did he choose to throw that up in my face?—They
worked and they made things, which is more than he's ever
done. Just carped at and criticized other people, who are
sweating blood to make something. Never mind, I'll show
him! Fashions change. You won't find many people, or public art galleries either, will want a whole room full of distorted
saucepans in assorted shades of blue and pink, with the paint
slapped on in lumps like a ploughed field. Long after he's
dead and buried, and his ideas with him, I'll be showing
him, and showing the world."

Tom held out his empty glass, blindly, in a trembling
hand. David took it from him. Tom stumbled towards the
door.

"I'm sorry," he muttered. "But you asked for it, and I
hope you like it now you've got it."

The Wintringhams exchanged glances. David quietly
turned the pages of the sketch book again, until he found
the drawing of Jill.

"May I have this one?" he asked, turning the book round
towards Tom.

The latter stopped to look back. Then nodded. He felt
exhausted, and curiously at peace. He had done something
outrageous, something that would have raised an uproar in
most of the houses he knew. Here it seemed to have been
accepted, and ignored; almost as if he had farted in public,
he thought.

"Right," said David. "Come along to my room and I'll
give you a cheque for it. I hope you don't want to put up
the price."

"Twelve, you said," Tom answered, in a low voice.

"Guineas," agreed David. He moved towards the door, opened it, and stood there, waiting.

Tom came to himself, suddenly. He thrust out a hand at Jill.

"I'll be saying good-bye then, Mrs. Wintringham."

He held her hand absent-mindedly, as he struggled to express himself. "I hope you didn't mind what I said just now. It means a lot to me. I mean, Chris is my friend. He's been pushed around an awful lot, and he can't take it. It worries me, what he might do——"

He broke off. Jill was looking at him sympathetically, but patiently. He understood that he was out of his depth, but he struggled on. "I don't want to embarrass you with our private affairs." This was terrible, he thought. It could mean all sorts of things he never intended. A sudden gleam of amusement shone in the calm grey eyes regarding him. He dropped Jill's hand, muttered "Thanks a lot for the sherry," and plunged out of the room. Jill put some more logs on the fire and sat down.

"You owe me a bob," said David, briskly, coming into the room ten minutes later.

"Beast! But I'm glad he came. I rather like him."

"He's all over the place, isn't he? I hope he settles down. Pity he has it in so, for Burke."

"I gathered it was chiefly the friend who really hated him."

"I'm not sure. Drummond was highly indignant on the friend's behalf. Looked at one stage as if he'd like to do Burke in with his own bare hands."

Jill said, bitterly, "I suppose you want to bet me another shilling he will?"

"Darling, you shock me."

"Well, that's quite an achievement, bet or no bet. I'll bet you a shilling he doesn't. And of course I'll win."

"You said that before."

Jill said, in a more serious voice, "Did you see that short paragraph in *The Times* this morning about the Westminster Gallery?"

"No. What about it?"

"A burglary. Not a very important one, or it didn't sound like it."

"Oh! What made you think of it just then?"

"We were talking about the place. Tom didn't mention it, did he?"

"No. Did you expect him to?"

"Yes. I waited to see if he would."

David shook his head impatiently.

"He was preoccupied with his drawing. Probably doesn't read newspapers."

"I just wondered."

"My dear girl, do you want to make another bet that Tom Drummond is a burglar?"

"Don't be silly, darling!"

Chapter III

THE next morning, at the Westminster Gallery, some workmen employed on the reconstruction of one of the exhibition rooms made a most unpleasant discovery.

This room was being redecorated, after the roof had been repaired and slightly altered. For some weeks visitors to the Gallery had heard the thump of heavy scaffolding being moved, and the monotonous hammering inseparable from all kinds of building work. They had not been able to see what was going on, because, though the doors of this room had been taken off their hinges, a large canvas screen had been hung in their place, to act as a dust excluder and partial muffler of noise, in neither of which functions was it strikingly successful.

Inside the room there was the usual chaos of a builder's site; dumps of materials, plaster in bags, paint in large drums, unused planks and trestles, boxes, and spare bundles of sacking and tarpaulin. Besides these, the usual camping site for the workmen, a semicircle of rough benches, made from used paint drums with boards on top, and surrounded by old discarded newspapers, football pool coupons, and cigarette ends and cartons.

It was near this tea-break encampment that the nasty find was made. The man whose duty it was to bring the tea up from the restaurant kitchen in the basement tripped over a loose bit of canvas, shaking some boiling water on to his wrist. He swore, set down the teapot carefully on the bench, and in a burst of anger seized the canvas and dragged it clear of the dump. Lying beneath it was the body of a man.

The workman, his anger absorbed in shock, let out a yell that brought those of his mates who were at ground level running over to see what was the matter. Two others, working on scaffolding higher up, saw plainly from their elevation the cause of the disturbance and came down in haste.

The foreman took action. That is to say he sent one of his men to report the find, and asked the unlucky discoverer if he had moved the body at all.

"Me touch that!" The man was yellow-faced and shaking. "Wot d'yer think?"

"There's one thing," said the foreman. "He didn't put himself under that dump. And there's another. It's been in this corner, the stuff and that, for the best part of a week, with none of us going near it. Correct?"

There was a murmur of agreement and approval. It was clear where the foreman's thought was directed. None of them was going to be involved. They knew nothing. Nothing whatever. That was the line. They knew nothing and they didn't want to know anything.

Following slowly along this unspoken line of argument the man who had made the discovery said, "We wasn't in 'ere at all yesterday, was we? Finishin' up that corridor back of this?"

The men agreed again.

"If I 'adn't of moved us over 'ere this morning, I wouldn't of found it."

"Why the 'ell did you want to move?" asked one indignant voice.

"Draught," answered the man. "Stan was complainin' 'e'd got a stiff neck in the draught from the door, over the other side."

"I never," repudiated Stan, embarrassed by the accusing eyes turned in his direction.

"It don't matter," said the foreman. "It'd have to be found sometime. Better now than later, in a way."

A sickly grin spread over one or two faces; others turned away. After a few minutes a stir at the doorway brought all the heads round in that direction. A gallery attendant, followed by a policeman, came in. They walked over to the group of workmen and stood looking down at the body in the dark suit powdered with dust. As they stood, not moving, a third man, obviously some official from the administrative side of the gallery, joined them. No one spoke for some time.

The body lay prone, the face hidden. Greying hair, well-cut, covered the back of the head. There was no obvious wound.

The policeman stepped forward, lifted a limp hand and let it fall. He gripped the dead man's shoulder, trying to peer at the hidden face, and as he did so the body's equilibrium shifted. It had been balanced on the pile of planks and sacking. The man who had uncovered it had, in tripping over part of the pile, moved it slightly. The policeman's action did the rest. Slowly, and as if deliberately, the dead man rolled over, showing them his face. The eyes were open, staring, fixed. The head was bent over, resting on the left shoulder.

The same evening Tom Drummond was leaning against the bar of his favourite pub, waiting for Pauline. She was late, as usual. But he had no doubt that she would eventually turn up. So he sipped at a meagre half-pint of brown ale, which was all he felt he could afford, and waited, ignoring the occasional attempts of his neighbours to start a conversation.

She was beside him before he noticed her arrival. He saw that she looked worried and pale.

"Late as usual," he grumbled, preferring his own grievance to her obvious distress.

She paid no attention to this, but ordered a beer for herself, and said nothing until she had it in her hand.

"Come away from the bar," she said then.

"Why?"

"Oh, don't argue! Something has happened. Something awful!"

Tom followed her wearily. Had she been thrown out of her digs again? She was an unlucky kid in this respect. Always quarrelled with her room-mates for one reason or

another. It would be awkward to have her back at the studio
with Chris in his present mood. Perhaps it wasn't the room.
Perhaps it was money. That would be easier. She didn't
know of his lucky break with the Wintringhams. He'd been
looking forward to telling her. But perhaps—— No, better
not think of that——

She found a place for them in a corner of the pub behind
a small table. As he sat down beside her she turned her
small pale face to him and asked slowly, "Have you seen an
evening paper?"

"No."

"I thought you couldn't have."

She did not seem able to go on. She just sat there, her big
dark eyes staring into his.

"Well," he said. "What's in it you thought I couldn't
have seen?"

Her face went a shade paler. She seemed all eyes, Tom
thought. He was beginning to feel anxious about her.
Surely nothing to do with Pauline could possibly be in an
evening paper.

She handed him the folded newsprint in her hand. It was
splashed with large type. He took it in very quickly.

"Art critic murdered. Body of Mr. Oswald Burke found
in the Westminster Gallery."

The pub swam before his eyes. He crushed the paper in
his hand and heard Pauline's voice in his ear.

"Drink something, for God's sake! People are looking at
you!"

This was not strictly true. She was looking at him, herself,
and looking intently, with a sickening confirmation of her
earlier fears. But no one else there had noticed the sudden
whitening of his face and stiffening of his body. Two young
people in a corner, even two young people as obviously strung
up as this pair, was nothing new in that place. Students.
There were hundreds thereabouts, going to the College and
the Art School. All much alike, and pretty harmless.

Tom did as she told him. Then he pushed the paper back
at her.

"Tell me about it," he said. "I expect most of it is a pack of lies."

She gave him the newspaper's account of the finding of the body.

"It says the neck was broken," she went on, with a tremulous disgust in her voice. "What can that mean?"

"Anything. Or nothing. They always exaggerate. Must have what they call a story. Sells the bloody paper. Does it say definitely it was murder? He didn't break his neck by accident?"

"It says evidence of foul play. They tie it in with the burglary."

"What burglary?"

"Don't you ever read the papers? Cash missing from a small safe. In yesterday's."

"Does it say when this chap was killed?"

"What do you mean? I've just told you. The burglar might have knocked him off."

"I saw him day before yesterday, at the Westminster. He was lively enough, then."

His manner shocked her.

"You hated him, didn't you?"

He gave a laugh that made her shrink away from him; some people at the next table looked round, disapprovingly.

"So that's your worry. You think I did it? Not this burglar?"

"I don't! Of course I don't!"

The dark eyes were filling with tears. Her lip trembled. Tom looked at her.

"Drink up," he said, curtly. "We'll get out of here."

He set the example by draining his own mug, then took her arm and pulled her to her feet.

They walked for about an hour, through the crowded, brightly lit streets, dodging the crowds, staring into shop windows, finally eating a sandwich and drinking coffee in a milk bar. After that Tom took Pauline back to her lodgings behind the Gray's Inn Road, where he said good night to her, and kissed her with a sudden, unexpected tenderness.

C

She watched him go. There had been no relief for her troubled mind. On their hectic tiring walk he had spoken very little, and not once of Oswald Burke and his terrible end.

The Wintringhams heard the news on the wireless the same evening. Their first thought, naturally, was of Tom Drummond.

"He couldn't have done it," Jill said, incredulously. "Surely he couldn't?"

"If he did it was before he came to see us. The chap said he was believed to have been dead at least thirty-six hours."

"It's twenty-four since Tom came here. The day before that we met him at the Gallery."

"And we met Burke there, too."

"Yes. How ghastly! Darling, Tom would never have come to see us as he did, with that on his conscience! It was the very next day!"

David got up.

"I think I'll try to get hold of Longridge. If they've called him in for the P.M. he may enlighten us."

"Don't you think you might leave it alone, darling? Just for once."

She knew it was hopeless, but she could not help it.

"Leave it alone, with that boy's sketch book full of most revealing portraits of a large number of people milling about the Westminster that afternoon? Not on your life. Always provided Burke was done in on Wednesday. That's what I want to ask Longridge."

The Home Office pathologist was at his own house and he had already performed an autopsy on the dead critic. The B.B.C. had not been given any details and so had not relayed them. David heard of them now with great disgust. He also heard that Burke had not, apparently, been seen since his visit to the Westminster on Wednesday of that week. Certainly he had not returned to his own home, but as his wife was away on a visit at the time, only now being called back, the housekeeper at his London home had concluded that he must have joined her without sending a message to that effect. There was one curious thing about the case. He proceeded to describe this to David.

The latter put down the receiver and went back to his place by the fire.

"You probably gathered most of that," he said.

"I gathered someone at Mr. Burke's house thought he had gone away. Also that there is something specially strange about the way he was killed."

"No. Not that. He was killed quite neatly and instantaneously, by a rabbit punch. His neck was broken. Longridge thinks he did not leave the Gallery that afternoon. No, the curious thing is about Symington-Cole."

"James?"

"Yes. It seems he turned up at the mortuary this afternoon when he'd seen the midday editions of the evening papers. He wanted the corneas. He'd got all the equipment to take them out."

"He wanted *what*?"

"Burke was a friend of his. He'd left him his corneas in his will. The cornea is the front part of the eye. No end of a fuss getting this verified with the lawyer and the wife and so on. James quite adamant. Furious the body hadn't been found earlier. Said his corneas—*his* corneas, mark you—were ruined: made no end of a fuss."

"I think he must be mad," said Jill.

"No. Only callous. Completely callous and one-tracked over his pet operation."

"Did Dr. Longridge let him have them?" Jill asked, shuddering.

"No point. Too late. But it was perfectly legal. Anyway, it couldn't hurt poor old Burke. He didn't need them any more. His idea, in leaving them to James, was the thought that they might help a blind man to see again."

"Because vision was the most important thing in life to him?"

"I think so."

They were silent for a time, then Jill said, "Who could have done it?"

"No idea. Have you?"

"No, of course not."

"You sound doubtful. Thinking of Tom Drummond?"

"Not him. The friend—what was his name—Christopher something."

"Felton."

David pulled his diary out of his pocket.

"Damn," he said, irritably. "I've got the address, but no telephone number."

"They'll tell you the number if you've got the name and address."

"If the 'phone is in his own name. Or Drummond's. Which I very much doubt."

David was right. The telephone inquiry operator wished to be helpful, but could not attach the address to any number.

"I'll have to go round," David said.

"Now?"

"The sooner the better."

He was gone about an hour, and came back still frustrated. Tom Drummond was out, people in the house told him. He and his friend were usually out in the evening, unless they were giving a party. There was disapproval in the tone in which this information was given.

"They are not over-popular at the place where they live."

"Where is it? You dashed off in such a hurry I didn't gather."

"Behind Mornington Crescent. Old houses, rather dilapidated. Let in floors, no stair carpet, general internal dinginess and dirt. I didn't see their rooms, which are on the top floor. They were locked up."

"What will you do now?"

"Wait till to-morrow. I might have a word with Steve."

"Poor Steve. He thinks you've retired from cutting in on him, as he calls it."

"Do him good to know I haven't. Not that I propose to do more in this case than persuade Tom Drummond to show them his drawing. There may be absolutely nothing in that for the Yard. In which case I step out of it again."

"Liar!" said Jill, tenderly.

Detective-Superintendent Mitchell was not at his home, David learned. He was at Scotland Yard. After a short delay he got through to him.

"Steve, are you, by any lucky chance, on this case of Oswald Burke?"

There was a groan from the other end of the line.

"Unfortunately, I am. Doubly unfortunately, if I've got you on my hands as well."

"You haven't. Not really. Not yet. I happened to be at the Westminster on Wednesday afternoon. With Jill."

"You would be. You saw it done, I suppose, but waited until the body was found to-day to speak up."

"No. I'm serious, Steve. I met someone there who might, just possibly, throw some light on it."

"Who?"

"I don't think I'll tell you that, now. It wouldn't be fair. I haven't contacted him, yet."

"It's a man, then?"

"Look. If I can get hold of him, and if he's willing to come, I'll bring him along to-morrow morning. That all right?"

"Anything's all right by me. For once the papers have the whole dope to date. By the way, Longridge is looking after that side."

"I know. I rang him up."

"You would. As usual everything falls into your lap, doesn't it?"

"Don't be bitter, Steve. Jill sends her love. See you to-morrow—perhaps."

Just before ten the next morning, David drove up to Scotland Yard. Tom Drummond, grim-faced and silent, hiding his inner consternation, got slowly out of the car and followed Dr. Wintringham into the building. With no delay at all they found themselves seated, one on each side of Superintendent Mitchell's desk.

David explained why he had brought Tom and who he was. The sketch book was handed over. Mitchell began to turn the pages. Then he stopped.

"There are several missing here," he said, looking up. "Why is that?"

"Well——" began David, with a sinking feeling, remembering what Tom had said of the drawing of the art critic. But he could not finish, for Tom leaned forward, cutting in.

"Dr. Wintringham took one of Mrs. Wintringham. And another of a doctor friend of his. That third gap was one of a man I—we—know. My friend—the man I share a studio with—he didn't like the way I'd done it. He tore it out."

David said nothing, but stretched out a hand and took the book from Mitchell. The sketches were all there as he remembered them, but he found he had forgotten whereabouts the ragged edge had come, the only ragged edge before he had taken out the drawings of Jill and Symington-Cole. He did remember, however, that on his last inspection he had not found the portrait of Burke that he had seen before at the Westminster Gallery. But now there was a drawing of him, a very striking piece of work indeed, something he could not possibly have missed. He handed the book back.

"Thank you," said Mitchell, dryly. "Do I take it you find someone missing since you saw it last?"

"No," said David, and left it at that.

"This is Burke," said Mitchell, turning the book round towards Tom, and watching him keenly. "It is recognizable from the photographs in life I have got, and it's more than that. You have accentuated the eyes, haven't you?"

Tom's pale face grew whiter, but his set expression did not change.

"I drew him looking at a piece of sculpture. That is how he looked at things. And at people, sometimes."

This last admission seemed to be dragged from him against his will. When he had made it, he stared at Mitchell, his mouth drawn into a hard line.

The Superintendent made no answer. Instead he turned the pages back to the beginning and began to go through them, one by one, writing down Tom's answers. David watched, checking this with what he remembered.

"A hall porter. A man and woman at the head of the stairs. I seem to know their faces."

He frowned, turning the book round to each of the others. David and Tom shook their heads. Sergeant Fraser, sitting behind Mitchell, said, "Cyril and Lily Ellis, sir."

"Who?" asked David.

"Television stars," said Mitchell. "Of course. I thought I recognized them."

He turned to the next page, repeating Tom's description, written underneath, "Two girls, looking at Ellen Standfast."

Not very respectfully, David thought. Mitchell said, "Dame Ellen Standfast was there that afternoon?"

"No. They were looking at the oil painting of her."

"I see. Gallery attendant. Now this gap. Who was that of?"

"Symington-Cole. I told you," said David. "I've got it here. He wants to see it, with a view to buying it."

He took the drawing from a large envelope he held, and gave it to Mitchell.

"That's the big eye surgeon, isn't it?" the latter asked. "The one that——" He left his sentence unfinished.

"Yes."

The word 'eye' struck them unpleasantly, for it lay uneasily that morning, for all of them, on the borders of horror and disgust. The police had not approved of Symington-Cole's behaviour in the mortuary.

"Yes," repeated Mitchell, who was looking at David. "I'll have a word with you on that, later."

The Superintendent turned another page and Tom supplied the name.

"Christopher Felton. The man I mentioned, who shares my studio. And the next one is him again with another friend of—ours, Hugh Lampton. He's a psychiatrist."

Mitchell glanced up, nodded, and went on again. There were more sketches, on some pages more than one figure, with perhaps a couple of heads as well, all put in with the economy of line, the certainty, that proclaimed Tom a born draughtsman, and already a master of his craft.

"Ah," said Mitchell, suddenly, taking a keener interest in what he saw. "And who may this be?"

"A workman. Connected with the alterations, I think. I jotted him down as I was leaving. He was crossing the hall."

"What time?"

"I don't know. Sixish."

"Where was he going?"

"Oh, for heaven's sake! I've just told you he was crossing the hall. I didn't speak to him. I was looking at the postcard reproductions, actually. He was not even near me."

"All right. You needn't get excited."

Tom bit back his next angry words. David looked across at him, shaking his head in silent disapproval and warning. Mitchell was showing the sketch book again to Sergeant Fraser.

"Got something?" David asked, quietly.

The Superintendent ignored this, addressing himself to Tom.

"I shall have to ask you to lend us these drawings of yours for a day or two."

"All right."

Tom gave his answer grudgingly, but without hesitation.

"Got something?" David asked again, as the sergeant left the room, taking the sketch book with him.

"Perhaps." Superintendent Mitchell stood up: it was clear that the interview was ended. But as he walked with them towards the main door of the building, Tom going ahead, he pulled David back and murmured, "Unless I am mistaken, or your young friend is less of a photographer than appears, that chap in the dungarees is an old friend of ours. A very old friend, indeed. And apropos of the empty safe at the Gallery, I've been actually thinking about him. This helps."

Chapter IV

DAVID drove to St. Edmund's from Scotland Yard. Tom Drummond had refused a lift, though the hospital was on the direct route back to his studio near Mornington Crescent.

"I don't happen to be going back there just now," he explained, ungraciously, when David pointed this out to him.

"My mistake. I hope to see Symington-Cole this morning or Monday. He's been away at some conference or other since Wednesday. Paris, I think."

"There's no particular hurry," said Tom. "He might want to think it over. Show it to other people or something."

"Good. I'll tell him that."

So they parted, and it seemed plain to David that Tom was not in any hurry to conclude the business they had in hand together, and this might mean one of several things. Though the lad obviously resented the whole idea of patronage, he was not averse to its obvious advantages in practice. By spinning out the Symington-Cole business he would keep in touch with the Wintringhams. Was this for the sake of his art? Or was it because he knew that David was a friend of Superintendent Mitchell?

Mitchell. It was annoying that Steve had impounded the sketch book. David would very much like to see it again. The question of those gaps. How many had there really been the first time he had looked at the book? Tom had torn out the one of Symington-Cole. Later he had also removed the one of Jill. They had discussed the ragged edges made by his friend Felton, who had taken and destroyed the very innocuous picture of Oswald Burke, drawn at the Gallery. Only, that first time in Hampstead, Tom said

he had torn it out himself. Impossible to know which story
to believe at the moment. That made three gaps. But this
morning in Steve's room there had been five. Well, there
was no reason why the boy should not tear up as much of
his work as he pleased. No reason at all. Only, it was odd
that he should have put in another picture of Burke, at the
end of the former series. And this since his visit to Hampstead, and therefore necessarily after the art critic's death.
From memory, then? Which might account for the curious
change in the whole presentation of the man. When he did
not know who he was, Tom had drawn him as a commonplace, kindly individual. After he knew, but not apparently,
on the same day, rather some two days later, he had shown
him with those remarkable, penetrating, luminous eyes. The
eyes that had been, in fact, quenched and dulled in death.
It was all very confusing, not to say sinister.

It being Saturday morning, David's work was light, no
lectures or official visits to the wards. He disposed of some
administrative problems; had a session with his secretary to
clear up the week's work from her point of view; looked into
the laboratory connected with his department to have a word
with one or two enthusiasts who took no account of time.
And with one reluctant worker, whose particular field needed
inspection just now at regular intervals, regardless of day or
night, week-day or week-end. Having seen what they were
all doing, encouraged them, pointed out possible snags, and
suggested how these might be overcome, he left the Medical
School for the hospital.

His main object was to find Symington-Cole. He knew he
was in the hospital, for the 'In' board said so. He rightly
judged that the great man would be in the eye ward. After
his absence at the conference, and in spite of his hurried
return, perhaps because of it, he would want to see how his
cases were getting on.

Symington-Cole, surrounded by a band of respectful, but
rather bored followers, was looking at a patient's right retina.
Bending close to the victim's head, his instrument held to
his own eye, he peered, indicated where the patient should

direct his own gaze, and peered again. Evidently this had been going on for some time. The students and the house-man, who could, of course, see nothing of any interest to them, fidgeted, shuffled their feet silently, looked at one another, winked, grimaced, but dared not speak. David joined the group, imposing, by his arrival, a new set of restraints, visual now as well as auditory. One onlooker, reaching the limits of endurance, tiptoed away, to be followed by two others. It seemed as if a rot might set in.

The houseman cleared his throat, as a preliminary to announcing David's arrival. The patient's eyes swivelled in his direction. He was more than fed up with staring into the distance at points indicated by the eye surgeon's waving finger. He would look at this new-comer and be damned to all pointless instructions.

Symington-Cole instantly waved his hand again, muttering testily, "Look at my finger. My finger, man! My finger!"

As there was no response he sighed and straightened his back, catching sight of David for the first time.

"Sorry," said the latter. "I'm afraid I'm interrupting."

"Quite all right," said the eye surgeon, irritably, adding in a calmer tone, "This is my last case for the morning."

He turned to his houseman. "Not more than three to examine, Cooper."

"No, sir."

The ward sister, who had been shaking up the patient's pillow, and settling him back comfortably on it, now soothed his growing indignation. The houseman allowed a student to step forward. The latter bent, adjusted his ophthalmo-scope, waved his other hand, and peered. The patient, with glazed eyes, blurred by atropine, stared dumbly into the distance.

Symington-Cole walked over to the wash-basins. David stood beside him, and handed him the towel when he needed it.

"I've got that sketch for you," he said. "Young Drummond will let you have it for twelve guineas."

"My wife was expecting to see it yesterday," said Symington-Cole. "She was disappointed. She had some friends along in the evening, and wanted to display it."

"I'm sorry," said David. "I couldn't get hold of Drummond to confirm with him that your wife definitely wanted it. He was out. I didn't see him till this morning. This business of Oswald Burke."

"Oh, that." Symington-Cole spoke coolly: too dispassionately altogether, David thought, for a man who had been chatting so amiably with the victim on the very day of his death. David went on, deliberately cool himself, to describe how he had shown the drawings to Superintendent Mitchell.

"You showed Scotland Yard a drawing of *me*?" exclaimed the surgeon, moved at last.

"Among others, yes."

"What right had you to do that?"

"Why should I not do it? I should have told them, in any case, that Jill and I had met Burke that afternoon, and that you introduced us. In any case you must have spoken to some of the police at the mortuary."

"Who told you I'd been at the mortuary?"

"Longridge."

"The devil he did! What business——"

Symington-Cole broke off abruptly and took the drawing from David, looking at it long and earnestly. This seemed to the latter a strange thing, but it showed him even more clearly what he had really known for some time, the essential, compelling egotism of the man.

The eye surgeon held out his hand for the large envelope in which the sketch had travelled. He tucked it inside, and then stood, turning it over and over, sunk in his own thoughts.

"I'll give you Drummond's address," said David, "then you can send him your cheque."

Symington-Cole roused himself.

"Do," he said.

He wrote it down on the envelope, and turned to go down the ward. David went with him. They walked along the corridor together to the lift.

"Burke was a thoroughly nice chap," said the eye surgeon suddenly, speaking with an effort. "I shall miss him terribly. We knew each other for a long time. I can't think that he ever had an enemy so bitter he'd wish him dead."

"Someone killed him."

"He was robbed, wasn't he?"

David stared. This had not been in the newspaper accounts that he had seen, nor had Mitchell told him anything about it.

"Do you know that?" he said.

"I was told his wallet and a gold cigarette-case had gone. I do know he always carried a good deal of cash with him."

"Who told you?"

"Longridge. Funny he told you about my being there, and didn't mention the thefts."

David had no answer to this, but he continued to be puzzled by the eye surgeon's ill-humour. His annoyance about the drawing could not have been that it told the Yard of his acquaintance with the murdered man, for he had already proved that to them by his presence at the mortuary and his purpose in going there. So it must have been something to do with the sketch itself. Perhaps Cole realized that it showed some aspects of his character usually concealed from the public gaze. If so, why did that matter?

The two men went down in the lift together, and together went into the staff cloakroom to get their coats and hats. On the way Symington-Cole switched the conversation to medical topics. They discussed David's various research projects briefly, and then turned to the eye surgeon's special field. It was plain that his apparent interest in David's work was only intended to lead up to this.

"You're lucky in having all the material you need ready to hand," he said, just before they parted on the steps of the hospital. "I'm hampered in my cornea work by the hopeless shortage of material. Can't get hold of enough corneas. The people who leave them in their wills often die so old they aren't any use when we get them. They are just as diseased as the ones they are meant to replace. It ought to be made legal to remove them compulsorily."

"All corpses to lose their corneas?"

"Not all. We don't want anything like all, of course."

"Blood donors are voluntary. There is no compulsion there, and we get plenty for transfusion. Publicity is what you want. A campaign in aid of."

"Not good enough. People give their own blood: it makes them feel good little heroes, or benefactors, anyway. Different to give something after you are dead. You can't appreciate the benefit. I don't see why relatives should not be asked to give the corneas. No man should have jurisdiction over his own corpse. It's a nonsense."

But a very deep-rooted one, David thought. Rooted in prejudice, perhaps, certainly in superstition; in ancient magic. If you took away a part of a dead man you took the power of the part. You took it for yourself, and you deprived his ghost of it. He did not say this aloud to Cole, but he did remark mildly, "Burke was an exception, then? An enlightened donor. Bad luck the corneas were not accessible to you when he died."

The eye surgeon's face darkened. He seemed about to explode again, but controlled himself, said good-bye brusquely, and turned away.

David stood on the steps of the hospital. He watched Symington-Cole get into his car and drive off. The keen, ruthless look on his thin face had never been more marked. He was a man of single purpose and great ambition, not so much for personal gain, though that came into it, but for his profession. His performance in his own field was brilliant, and he was very vain, but he would never be satisfied merely with a superb display of skill in all the conventional operations. He was perpetually extending their field. Corneal operations were his special interest. But how far was he prepared to go to overcome the known shortage he complained of? David saw where his thoughts were taking him and pulled himself up sharply. If Symington-Cole was capable of going to such length, he was mad, certi-

fiably mad. Besides, it was unlikely, if he brought himself
to kill Burke, that he would leave the corneas until after the
body was found, knowing that in all probability they would
be spoiled by the time-lag, as had, in fact, happened. All
the same, he decided to ask Superintendent Mitchell whether
it was true that Oswald Burke had been robbed, and if so,
how the eye surgeon had come to know this. He did not
believe the Home Office pathologist would give away that
kind of information.

He got into his own car and drove off, determined to settle
the point at once. He found Mitchell at the Yard, and put
it to him.

"Oh, yes, that's all right," the Superintendent told him.
"He rang up last night to say he'd been away at a conference
but had been with Mr. Burke at the Westminster that afternoon, so we asked him to come in and tell us what he could.
I asked him whether Burke had been wearing a watch and so
on, and he described the cigarette-case and the wallet and
then asked me straight out if they'd gone. It was pretty
obvious to him they had from the questions I asked him.
There seemed to be no point in denying it."

"I wonder why he told me it was Longridge he'd got the
information from."

"Perhaps he didn't want to be thought eager to give us
any information."

"Why not? He was a friend of Burke's. The Press didn't
get the robbery, did they? Wasn't it a bit rash to tell
Cole?"

"I told you. He'd guessed it already. Besides, the Press
aren't always as clever as they like to make out. And there
had been this safe-breaking. The Press want to tie the two
things together. Cole didn't want publicity; he wouldn't
give them anything. And they'd been warned to be careful
of Burke's reputation. He was an important figure, you
know."

"Of course I know. Was there anything the matter with
his reputation?"

"Absolutely nothing. But he was an odd character, always

slanging young artists in print, and doing them good turns in private."

"Oh, I see. Rather tricky."

"Once or twice the more dirty-minded gossip writers tried to make something of it. They were warned off. Actually, their editors mostly had more sense than to take up that line, however carefully."

"I see," said David again.

He went back to his car, stopped at a call box and rang up his home to tell Jill he would not be back to lunch. Then he drove on to Oswald Burke's house in Kensington.

Mrs. Burke was in, and consented to see him. He began by apologizing for his intrusion.

"But I know you," she said. "Or rather, I know of you. Jim Cole is an old friend of ours. He has often mentioned you when he was telling us about St. Edmund's. And then, naturally, we have heard of your more public work."

"It is in my public character that I have come to see you now," said David. Inwardly, he was amused to hear the eye surgeon referred to as Jim Cole, and wondered if the Symington had perhaps only acquired its hyphen as the owner rose in eminence. But his face showed nothing of this. The look he turned on Mrs. Burke was grave.

"Quite by chance I met your husband with Symington-Cole at the Westminster on Wednesday afternoon. My wife and I had a few words with him. Then, later, I found myself in possession of some facts that could be of use to the police, and as I know one of the Scotland Yard Superintendents personally, I took these facts to him. He had already taken over the case."

"What facts?" asked Mrs. Burke.

She was strangely self-possessed, David thought, for a woman so swiftly and tragically widowed. There were lines of strain about her mouth, and dark shadows under her eyes, but no trace of recent tears, nor any tremor in her quiet voice. Still, she looked about sixty, and well-bred women of her generation kept their emotions to themselves in public,

D

and before strangers. The stronger the feeling, the more ruthlessly it would be repressed. It was wrong to conclude that she might be heartless.

He told her briefly about Tom Drummond's sketches and how they might possibly be useful to Superintendent Mitchell. She nodded, but looked inquiring.

"I am sure you did not come to see me simply to tell me this," she said.

"No. I came to ask you if you knew of anyone who could be considered a dangerous enemy of your husband."

"No," she answered, without hesitation. "There were a good many people in his profession who did not agree with him. Some of them thought his views extreme, or else mistaken. But differing views are the stock in trade of critics. They would be very unlikely to kill someone who disagreed with them. It would destroy so much good material for their own work."

She smiled faintly, and again David marvelled at her apparent detachment. It helped him, however, to make his next move.

"Then, if that is impossible, and of course I agree with you that such a melodramatic event is most unlikely, would it be possible for him to have another kind of enemy, one whom he hated, rather than the other way round?"

The faintest possible shadow came into Mrs. Burke's eyes. In place of control, there was now a definite withdrawal.

"If that were so," she said, and the even tones of her voice were unaltered, "surely one would expect a very different event."

Meaning that Burke would have killed rather than been killed, David concluded. He drove his ideas into the open.

"It occurred to me that he might have hated someone with good cause, and warned that individual, who lost his head and killed him."

"Warned him of what?" she asked.

He was baulked. He said, brutally, "I suppose there was no chance your husband was being blackmailed?"

"*Blackmailed!*" This aroused great indignation, but

nothing more. " Oh, I see. You have been told about the
newspaper articles last year. You see I give you credit for
not having *read* the gutter press. Our solicitor dealt with
that. There were only two that could have had an offensive
meaning. They were stopped. There was a settlement out
of court, which was not even reported in the papers. It was
a disgraceful thing, of course. My husband was so kind to
all these young artists. He gave them so much personal
encouragement. I have listened to him talking about them
for hours at a time."

" He was not always encouraging," said David. " Very
often he was exactly the opposite."

" Only when he felt they were wasting their time, or
deliberately trying to put across something false."

" A lot of people think he encouraged work that is funda-
mentally false or decadent."

" That is a matter of opinion," said Mrs. Burke, coldly.

" I'm sorry. We must not discuss art. For one thing I
know too little about it. But there is this point about
students and other artists whom he antagonized. I'm not
suggesting any one of them felt so extremely that he would
be prepared to do murder in revenge for his hurt feelings.
But artists are often unstable, excitable people. Can you
think of any of those who ever came here, who might, in a
fit of mental instability, do such a thing? "

She paused before answering, evidently going over in her
mind all those of her husband's casual visitors she could
recollect.

" No," she said at last. " No one."

" Tom Drummond never came here? " He described Tom
briefly, adding that the lad felt very bitter about Burke's
criticism of his work.

" No. I don't remember that name, or anyone of that
description."

" Nor his friend, Christopher Felton? Thin face, black
beard? "

She smiled faintly for the second time.

" So many of them had thin faces and black beards. But

no, I don't remember him, either.   He would not be likely
to come if they were not friends.   All the ones who came
were devoted to my husband."

They were back where they had started, with no gain, and
the same questions left in the air.   David thanked her and
went away.   It had been less trying than he had feared, but
also less rewarding.   However, one thing had emerged, or
rather one suggestion.   Oswald Burke had known someone
whom he considered an enemy: Mrs. Burke had not wished
to disclose anything about this person, and it seemed improbable that the enemy had any connection with her husband's
profession of art critic.

With this meagre result David went home to Jill, unsatis-
fied.   There was nothing more he could do at present.   He
decided to give up trying for the rest of the week-end.

Chapter V

DAVID was as good as his word. He took no further action in the case that day, nor on the Sunday that followed. Instead he made sure of it by taking Jill into the country for the day. They drove out through Henley to the Thames near Wallingford, ate sandwiches in the sun on the top of Sinoden Hill, and sat there, sheltered by the great dyke of the ancient settlement, looking down on the silver loop of the river at Day's Lock, and the distant tower of Dorchester ※ away on the flat land to the north. They found tea in one of the few shops at Windsor that were open so early in the year, and then drove home.

Nanny came out into the hall when she heard them arrive. "There's been a telephone call," she said. "Wanting to speak to one of you. She didn't say which."

"She?"

"It sounded like a young woman, by the voice. Gave the name of Miss Manners."

"I don't know anyone called Manners. Do you, David?"

"Might be a patient, I suppose. But I can't place it. My memory for names gets worse every day."

"She didn't sound like a patient, doctor," said Nanny. "She left a number in case you cared to ring her back. Those were the words she used."

Nanny's voice implied that they were not the words she would use herself. Having delivered the message, she turned away.

"I'm afraid we're a bit late," Jill apologized.

Perhaps Nanny was offended by this, which would account for her unusually abrupt manner. But the old woman looked back and smiled.

"Oh, no, you're not. My sister doesn't expect me till

※ The one in Oxfordshire

seven. I told her I wouldn't be leaving here much before a quarter to."

Jill felt relieved.

"Well," she said, looking at her watch, "it's very nearly that, now. You'd better get going, hadn't you? "

Nanny smiled again, and went away.

"Better ring up the mysterious stranger," said David.

"Shall I? In case it's a patient that needs heading off? "

"Right. Go ahead."

The number was engaged, so the Wintringhams left it at that for the moment. Nanny went out, unhurried but purposeful, to pay her usual Sunday visit to her sister, who lived in Kilburn. Jill got supper. They had just finished the washing up afterwards when the telephone-bell rang.

"I'll go," Jill said. "It's probably our unknown caller."

It was. A girl's voice asked for Dr. Wintringham. Jill explained who she was, and waited.

"Mrs. Wintringham? " the voice said. "Oh, I see. Well, perhaps I could see you instead."

"See me? " said Jill. "You haven't even told me who you are. What do you want to see us about? "

"I'm sorry," the voice went on, slightly resentful. "I haven't had much chance to explain, yet, have I? "

Jill felt inclined to put down the receiver, but she controlled her impatience, and instead told the speaker to go ahead.

"I'm Pauline Manners," the girl told her.

"Pauline Manners? " Jill echoed, unenlightened.

"I'm a friend of Tom Drummond's."

"Oh," answered Jill. "Why didn't you say so right off? I thought it might be a patient, and I didn't want my husband bothered on a Sunday evening with inquiries that ought to be made at the hospital. Do you specially want to speak to him? "

"It depends. Frankly, I'd much rather talk to you. I think I'd be scared of Dr. Wintringham."

There did not seem to be an answer to this, so Jill waited.

"Hullo, are you there? I said I'd rather talk to you if I may."

"Yes."

"You mean I can?"

Jill made up her mind.

"I can't see you to-night. It's too late. But if you like to come here sometime to-morrow morning. Is Mr. Drummond with you? Has he given you the address?"

"Yes. No. I mean, he gave me your address. That's how I found the 'phone number. But he isn't here. He hasn't been all day. I expect he's gone home—to Colchester. I haven't seen him since Friday, actually."

The girl's voice grew husky as she said this, and Jill felt sorry for her.

"Don't worry," she said, kindly. "Come and see me to-morrow morning. I'll have some coffee brewing about eleven."

"Oh, thank you, Mrs. Wintringham. I hope you didn't mind me ringing you. I——"

"Of course I don't mind," said Jill, firmly. "See you to-morrow."

She put back the receiver before the girl could start on any fresh explanations. When she turned round she saw David, lying back in his armchair, looking at her.

"What are you grinning at?" she asked, going over to him. He put out an arm to pull her down to his knee.

"Was that Tom's girl?" he asked.

"How did you guess? I only said his name once."

"You repeated hers. He told me he had a girl-friend called Pauline."

"I see. The atrocious memory at work? Why didn't you come and take over from me?"

"You seemed to be getting on so nicely. She was worried about Tom, I suppose?"

"Yes. What shall I do if she tells me he did it?"

"Hand her on to Steve. But she won't."

" Are you so sure he didn't do it? "

" No. But I'm perfectly sure he wouldn't let her know if he had."

" I wonder why he has run away? "

She slipped lower on his knee until her head rested on his shoulder.

" Oh, come, come," he said. " Surely a chap can spend a week-end with his people in East Anglia without being suspected of murder? "

" Even if he doesn't tell his girl-friend he is going? "

" Certainly. How do we know she is the only girl-friend? Or even the chief one? "

" We don't. I wish I hadn't landed myself with her for to-morrow morning."

" That's the worst of having a kind heart, my darling. But I wouldn't have you any different."

" Don't be so smug. You know you're just pleased I'm doing your dirty work for you."

Pauline Manners turned up at the Wintringhams' house exactly on time at eleven the next morning. Jill opened the door to her ring, and Nanny brought the coffee-tray into the drawing-room three minutes later.

Miss Manners had not copied Tom Drummond in the matter of dress, Jill noticed. She had made no effort at formality; she had not put on the equivalent of the suit he had worn. Her clothes were of the ubiquitous, casual type; very narrow tartan slacks and a loose black jacket over a loose emerald green sweater. Her straight hair was scraped back and tied in a mare's tail that swung well below her shoulders. She had on white cotton socks and little flat black slippers. Her make-up, however, was not excessive, and her nails were unpainted. In fact, her hands had a distinctly grubby, roughened look about them.

" Do you paint as well? " Jill asked her, thinking this might account for the hands.

" Yes. Design is what I'm keen on." Seeing Jill's blank face, she went on, " I'm doing a general course at present.

But I want to design for textiles or pottery. There's quite a big field."

"Commercial art?" Jill asked.

Pauline nodded.

"There are very good openings. I suppose you think it's inferior, wanting to work commercially?"

"No, I don't. I think it's very sensible, and—and desirable. The more talent that goes into making patterns for decoration, the better."

"I haven't got all that much talent," said the girl, frankly. "But I'll get by."

"I'm sure you will. Come and sit down and tell me about Tom Drummond."

But Pauline, coffee-cup in hand, moved away from her, to stand by the window, looking out into the garden.

"This is a lovely house," she said, in a low voice. "I didn't know—I expect you think it's pretty awful of me, crashing in on you."

"No," said Jill. "Of course I don't. Perhaps it will be easier if I ask you a few questions, first. When did Tom give you our address, if you haven't seen him since Friday?"

Pauline answered, without turning round.

"On Thursday, I think it was. I meet him most nights. He was thrilled because Dr. Wintringham bought that drawing of you."

She turned round, and smiled slowly.

"I can see how good it was. I thought it was lovely when I was looking at the book on Wednesday."

"Ah," said Jill. "You met him on Wednesday evening, just as usual?"

"Yes. Oh, I see what you mean!"

The cup clattered in the saucer as she put it down. Jill said gently, "Do come and sit over here. You're all strung up."

Pauline gave in. She sat down, she let her cup be filled again, and then she began to talk. Jill sat and listened.

There was very little substance in the girl's account of the last few days, but Jill gained one or two definite impressions.

Tom had been very subdued on Wednesday, after his initial excitement over the Wintringhams' invitation. His thoughts were elsewhere. But Pauline took no notice, because he was often like that when he had been to an exhibition. He was late meeting her, but that again could happen. On Thursday he had been elated, full of the visit he had just made to Hampstead, and wondering when he would get further news of the Symington-Cole sketch.

"Mr. Cole was away," Jill explained. "He only saw the drawing for the first time on Saturday. But he wanted it at once. He has definitely bought it."

Pauline looked relieved and went on with her tale. She described Tom's alarming behaviour on Friday night, and his subsequent, still unexplained, absence.

"It isn't that I think he had anything to do with it," she cried, passionately. "He could never think of such a ghastly thing. It just is that he's acting so strangely, and it's dangerous for him. The police are such fools."

"Not always," corrected Jill, smiling. "We know one of them very well. And my husband has worked with them a lot."

Pauline looked bewildered. Evidently she had not heard of David's occasional excursions into police investigation. Jill enlightened her.

"You mean Dr. Wintringham is actually on this case himself?"

"Not in any way officially. He never is. But he often gets the answer first."

"Oh." Pauline was a good deal put out. She sat looking at Jill reproachfully, so that the latter felt moved to say:

"You came here off your own bat, didn't you?"

"Fair enough. But I think you might have warned me before I began to talk about Tom."

"You have said nothing against him, or that could be turned against him. *I* don't think it's strange for him to go away for the week-end. Very likely he sees he is in a slightly difficult position, and wants to ask his father's advice."

"They don't get on much together," said Pauline,

gloomily. "If he's really in trouble with the police he'll only get a rocket from the old man."

"Surely not?"

"You don't know them! They think Tom's wasting his time at the Art School. They grudged him every penny he needed over and above the State scholarship. So he stopped taking it from them. Now they're on at him for being so independent, and not having enough money to get any decent clothes."

"He was quite well-dressed when he came here," said Jill.

"I know. That's his only suit, and he's had it for years. His mother spends the earth on her clothes. The flashy cheap kind, but lots of them. And costume jewellery, you wouldn't credit! I don't believe Tom ought to have the State scholarship at all, now. I'm sure his father is over the income limit. If he was a doctor or a lawyer, or Tom had been to a public school, they'd be down on him to take it away. Just because his dad was in a small way when Tom was at his primary school, there are no questions asked."

"You don't like Tom's people?"

"They don't like me," said the girl, with a sudden quick laugh. "They think he ought to go about with class. There are some at the School, of course."

Jill laughed, too, and then, becoming serious again, asked why exactly Pauline had wanted to see her.

"Chiefly to find out if you and Dr. Wintringham think Tom is in real danger."

"You mean of being accused of the murder, or of being arrested? Well, I don't think he can be. And I shouldn't think my husband does, either. Nor Superintendent Mitchell, our friend at the Yard. As far as I know he was very pleased that Tom came forward with the sketch book."

"There's another thing," said the girl, slowly, and Jill realized that now they were coming to the root of her anxiety. "It's his friend, Chris Felton. Did he tell you about Chris?"

"He shares the studio, doesn't he?"

"That's right. Mrs. Wintringham, he's a real stinker. He's bad for Tom. I know he is. Him and his mother, both."

"You don't seem to like any of Tom's connections, do you? Neither his relations, nor his friends?"

The girl's face grew crimson, and her dark eyes flashed.

"It isn't jealousy, if that's what you mean! But Chris is a real menace, moaning all day and never doing a stroke of real work. I wish he'd go, only Tom can't afford the rent of the studio on his own. Chris knows it, and so does that mother of his. She puts up the money, you see."

"All right," said Jill, patiently. "So you hate Mr. Felton and his indulgent mamma. What has that got to do with the present crisis?"

"*He* might have done it," said Pauline, bluntly, and sat staring at Jill.

The latter stared back. She remembered Tom Drummond's words about his friend. That he might be driven by his frustrations into doing something terrible. Was this what he meant? Murder?

"And if he has?" she asked, steadily.

"I want to go round to the studio," said Pauline, completely frank at last. "To see if Tom's back. I rang, and only Chris answered. He just said, 'Go to hell!' and rang off. So I don't know if Tom is there or not. And I daren't go, because if it's only Chris, and he did it, he might go for me, too. I expect you think I'm cracked, but I truly believe Chris is, and I'm scared. I can't help it!"

Large tears filled the big dark eyes and rolled out down Pauline's cheeks. She did nothing to stop them.

"Well," said Jill, "let's go along there together, shall we?"

Pauline stopped crying immediately.

"Would you really?" she asked.

"Why not?" said Jill. "We'll go at once. I'm afraid my husband has the car, but we can go by Tube. That'll be quickest. Mornington Crescent, isn't it?"

"This is terribly good of you, Mrs. Wintringham."

"No. It's mainly curiosity. And wanting to be one up on David. Now, I'll go and get a coat."

She moved to the door and opened it.

"If you want to spend a penny, the downstairs aunt is the first door beyond the stairs, on the right."

The house behind Mornington Crescent was very much what Jill expected from David's description, only dingier and more dilapidated. It seemed to belong to an elderly couple, living on the ground floor, who spied on them from beside mangy brown velveteen curtains as they stood on the doorstep. After ringing the bell marked Felton several times, Jill made signals to the two interested faces. Whereupon the female one withdrew, and presently appeared again in the open doorway.

"Thank you," Jill said, taking charge of the situation. "Can you tell me if Mr. Felton's bell is working?"

This was not the question the woman was expecting, and she was surprised into speaking the truth.

"I couldn't say, I'm sure. But 'e's up there, that I do know. Come down for the milk an hour or so back, and 'is ma's with 'im. She 'as a key, see?"

"Thank you," said Jill, "then we'll go up."

She moved forward, and the woman moved back, and they were both inside the house.

"I don't undertake to open no doors," said the woman, recovering from the shock of this rapid defeat. "You might tell 'im that, from me. If 'e wants to keep the place on."

Jill made no answer to this, which did not in the least concern her, but began to walk upstairs, followed by Pauline, admiring and slightly envious. What you couldn't put over with that sort of nerve! Just sailed in, and made it look as if the old faggot had invited her. Could you beat it!

"That's the landlady," she whispered, on the next landing. "Proper old tartar!"

"I wonder if the bell really did ring," Jill answered. They completed the climb in silence.

Pauline knocked on one of the two doors on the top landing, which was the third floor of the house. A woman's voice said, "Come in."

The room was large, and attic-shaped, with a skylight, and another window in the front wall. One end of the room was filled with the usual junk of an artist's trade, easels, canvases, and semi-theatrical properties of various kinds. At the other end of the room, grouped beside a closed stove, were a few comfortable chairs and a divan covered with a loose piece of crimson brocade, very much the worse for wear. Among the cushions on this divan reclined the young man with the black beard whom Jill had seen at the Westminster Gallery. A woman sat beside him, her plump body perched on the edge of the divan. She wore a glossy fur coat, and had a bright turquoise satin flower-pot, wreathed in spangled tulle, set on her grey curls. She was looking eagerly towards the door, but as Pauline stepped forward, Jill saw the round face change.

"What right——?" she began, but Jill, following Pauline, stopped her.

"This is Mr. Drummond's flat, isn't it?" she asked, gently.

Christopher Felton sat up. Pauline said, nervously, "This is Mrs. Wintringham, Mrs. Felton. She and Dr. Wintringham know Tom. We came to see——"

"He isn't here," said Christopher, interrupting his mother's unwilling acknowledgment of Jill.

"Why didn't you say so when I rang up?" Pauline demanded.

"But he's coming back to-night," Felton went on. "He wrote a note."

"You might have said."

"I might. And I didn't. So what?"

"So we had to come and find out," said Pauline, with spirit.

"Did he say when, exactly?" Jill asked.

Mrs. Felton began to bluster.

"I don't know what it is to you, Mrs.—er—Wintringham,"

she began. "That girl is always in and out. Makes herself a perfect nuisance. If Tom wants to get away from her for a few days, I'm not at all surprised. But I can't see why she should bring a perfect stranger, with Chris not at all well——"

"I'm all right," the young man muttered, rudely. "You shut up."

He got off the divan and stood up, stretching himself and yawning.

"Let's get the hell out," he said. His mother stood up obediently.

"Well, really!" she protested again. But something in Jill's quiet indifference checked a fresh outburst, and she stopped, nervously settling her hat and pulling her fur coat round her.

Christopher Felton stood at the door until his mother was through it. Then he tossed a crumpled bit of paper towards Pauline.

"It was addressed to you," he said. "But I opened it."

He was gone, banging the door behind him before Pauline could loose an indignant cry. She stood, speechless with anger, Tom's note to her in her hand. She could hardly see the writing through her tears of rage and mortification.

'Darling,' it began, 'I am sending this to the studio as I don't want you mixed up in it, as you might be if I addressed it to your digs. You never know who will open letters——'

"You don't, do you?" she said, aloud. "Tom wants me to meet him as usual, to-night. So it's all right so far, thank God."

"But this isn't," said Jill.

She had a sheet of drawing paper in her hand. It had been lying under the cushion that had supported Christopher Felton's unkempt head. On the paper was a drawing of Oswald Burke, not the mild caricature she had seen at the Gallery, nor the strange portrait David had described to her after his visit with Tom to Scotland Yard. In this latest sketch the commonplace character of Burke's features was exaggerated into a brutish stupidity, while the eyes, prominent, staring fiercely, held an unexampled malignant ferocity that made her catch her breath.

"There is nothing right about this," said Jill.

And Pauline, white and shaken, could only nod her head, agreeing.

Chapter VI

MEANWHILE Scotland Yard had not been idle. Superintendent Mitchell seized upon the one reasonable clue offered him, and at once set in motion the very formidable machine of investigation.

"Yes, it's Bert Lewis all right," he said to Sergeant Fraser, when he returned to his office after seeing David and Tom leave the Yard.

They were comparing Tom's sketch with the photographs in the file. The likeness was unmistakable.

"It's not an uncommon face, all the same," said the sergeant, thoughtfully. He distrusted the power of the human hand, compared, say, with the lens of a good camera.

"Taken by itself, before comparison, I spotted it and you agreed," insisted Mitchell. "This young chap has a gift for likenesses we can't deny. I don't see why we shouldn't consider it as evidence. In this particular case it's better than a verbal description, after all, and we rely on those."

Sergeant Fraser still had misgivings, but he kept them to himself. A plan of campaign was laid out.

To begin with the foreman of the works contractors at the Westminster Gallery was asked about his team. The work was still in hand there, when the police officers called, though the morning was well advanced, and being Saturday, work was due to end at twelve. In order to prove his own point about the drawing, Mitchell produced this first of all. The foreman had no hesitation in naming it.

"Forbes," he said. "I took him on temporary, a couple of weeks back, for a chap that had gone sick. He was paid off, Forbes, I mean, and got his cards back last Saturday."

"*Last* Saturday?"

"That's what I said. We're working overtime on this lot."

The foreman began to look sullen, but Mitchell pressed on, ignoring the explanation.

"Then he wasn't here, or rather he wasn't working, on Wednesday this week?"

"No. He wasn't working here after last Saturday. Like I told you. He was paid off, and got his cards——"

"I see. What time do you pack it in daily?"

"Five-thirty."

"Your men actually leave the building at five-thirty? Have knocked off actual work about fifteen minutes earlier, I suppose?"

The foreman nodded. His expression suggested that this ruddy dick could suppose anything he mucking well liked. Mitchell, knowing the look well, went on to other matters.

"What sort of work was this man you called Forbes doing?" he asked.

"Unskilled. General labourer."

"Remember which Exchange you got him from?"

"No, I don't. I didn't trouble much about him. I wanted a pair of hands till my own man came in again, and I'd got them. He did what he was asked, and kept himself to himself, as you might expect with a temporary."

Mitchell left him and went out on to the Embankment. There was no point in going over the discovery of the murder again with the foreman. His statement and those of the men concerned had been taken the day before and would be given again on Monday at the inquest.

He had been able to get nothing definite from the staff in the hall or the attendants in the various rooms of the Gallery. The girl behind the circular display of postcard and other reproductions, books, and pamphlets, had noticed Tom, but she had not noticed any particular workman crossing the hall. They were crossing it all day long, she explained. But not after five-thirty, Mitchell suggested. The girl reddened, but stuck to her position of total ignorance. Probably too set on watching Tom, whose looks would be sure to attract female attention, thought the Superintendent. Perhaps she was so set on catching his eye, and even his pencil, that she was blind to any other event in her neighbourhood. Besides, the workmen were no concern of hers, as she had already made plain to him. The porters had professed an equal lack of observation and interest.

"Wouldn't be likely to notice him," said one. "He would certainly not leave by this door."

"Which one, then?"

"You'd better ask the foreman. He'll be able to tell you."

As Mitchell had already been shown the side door the workmen used, and had only wanted to test the porter's knowledge of their habits, he had not pursued this suggestion.

He leaned on the parapet, looking across the river to the south bank. It was clear now that Bert Lewis, incorrigible petty thief and small-time burglar, was back at his favourite pastime, after two or three years of good behaviour. Or, perhaps, of just not being found out. The temporary job must have been a great temptation, unless it was a deliberately taken chance of having a good look round. It was all too easy. Slip in by the main door, respectably dressed, bringing a pair of dungarees hidden under his overcoat. Put them on in a lavatory or some remote part of the large building. Walk unobtrusively into the room under reconstruction and hide there until the public galleries closed at seven. When the day staff had left, he would have the place to himself, except for night watchmen.

It was a familiar set-up, Mitchell thought, watching the gulls swooping down to attack a piece of garbage floating upstream on the tide. And it had worked out like that. A safe blown, not very skilfully. All the signs of Lewis's inept handiwork. But, in addition, a corpse, thirty-six hours dead when found, and robbed of money and valuables.

He sighed. They so often came to this in the end. Some unfortunate blighter interrupted them, and, in a sudden burst of fear and rage, was put out to stop his mouth. No one would ever know why Burke had wandered off into that part of the building. Just part of his general curiosity and keenness over anything remotely connected with Art? Mitchell had heard from David Wintringham that the most heated arguments went on, even about such things as the correct hanging of pictures, the background that should be provided for them, both the colour and texture of wall covering and so on. Burke probably went behind the screens to investigate what was going forward. The attendants would not look for anyone there; when the rooms open to the public were empty, they would naturally conclude that all the visitors had left. And then Lewis, exasperated at this check to his plans, or perhaps himself discovered lurking there with obviously evil intent, had taken the quick, but fatal, way out. All the same, there was a snag, a very serious snag.

For violence of any kind, on the part of little Bert Lewis, was highly improbable, Mitchell told himself, impatiently. Particularly such a neat, exact killing. That wasn't an argument. No one knew the form for Bert, because this was the first time he had killed. If he had. The provocation would be strong, if in fact Burke had got in his way. Bert's last sentence had been six years' preventive detention. Another conviction might send him down for ten. He was now over fifty. A sentence like that would be the end of him, and he knew it. It would look much the same to him as that numerically longer, but, with remissions, not effectively much worse sentence he might now expect, instead of being hanged. Twenty-five years, which meant fifteen, as against ten. But he would be an old man whichever it was, so why not take the chance, if he could make a clean getaway.

That was how Bert might have argued, if he had had time to argue with himself at all. And that was what might be going to happen to him.

But first he had to be found, Mitchell reminded himself. And also some real evidence of his guilt.

The machine moved slowly. The week-end intervened, during which nothing could be done at the Labour Exchanges. They could look round Bert's usual haunts, ask the usual narks, but it was not till Monday that serious inquiries could start up. This was the day on which Jill Wintringham had gone with Pauline to the studio in Mornington Crescent.

By Tuesday, Bert, under his latest alias of Forbes, was traced to the Labour Exchange that had supplied him to the Westminster Art Gallery. He had not registered at this Exchange before, but his cards were in order.

"Of course the address in Wandsworth he gave there had never heard of him," reported Sergeant Fraser, later.

"Naturally," said Mitchell. "I didn't think we'd get much that way. But it shows he hasn't changed his technique. He was always a great hand at false cards. Trouble is he seems to have gone straight, or straight enough, for so long. We've rather lost sight of him."

"Approach the usual channels?" asked Fraser, with pompous formality.

"Jump in and swim along them," answered Mitchell, with a grin. "You'll find them in the Deptford, Greenwich and Lewisham area. That's where he's always lived. You'll find the places in the file where he has actually had digs. He won't be at any of them, but somebody might have a down on him, and grab the chance to get even. He's a mean bastard to his associates; that's why he's always worked alone for the last fifteen years."

"Have to try everything, won't we?" said Sergeant Fraser, cheerfully. He was young and enthusiastic, and for him routine had not yet palled.

"You do that," agreed Superintendent Mitchell.

For himself, he had other plans. There was one person that Sergeant Fraser would not know how to handle, and this was Bert Lewis's wife. To Superintendent Mitchell she was one of the most extraordinarily courageous women he had ever come across. Big, energetic, with an indomitable optimism and a cast-iron constitution, she had ridden over all the formidable obstacles in her path without seeming to suffer either hardship or loss. Her easy tolerance embraced all of Bert's shortcomings including his long absences, sometimes enforced, sometimes of his own choosing. She cleaned offices for a living, and provided her two children with ample food and clothing, and with unceasing warm affection, if with no very marked moral standards. Superintendent Mitchell both admired and liked her, and she liked the Superintendent, as far as a normal person could ever like the hand of authority, because he never bullied her, and always told her the truth about Bert, however bad it might be.

Mrs. Lewis, at this present time, lived in Camberwell, in one of a cluster of ageing prefabs, not far from the Green. Her children still lived at home, though the boy was away just now doing his National Service in the north of England, and the girl was out all day, undergoing a secretarial training on a public grant. She possessed all of her father's quick wits and ingenuity, combined with her mother's stamina, and promised to go far. Mrs. Lewis was justly proud of her.

Superintendent Mitchell called at the prefab early on Monday afternoon. He knew that the office cleaning took place between seven and nine in the morning, and five and eight in the evening. Cleaning at the local cinema occupied the two hours from ten until noon. In the early part of the afternoon Mrs. Lewis would be occupied with her own affairs, and on Monday these would be the weekly wash.

He was right. Mrs. Lewis, her big arms red from the soapy hot water, was hanging out clothes and bed linen on the line in her tiny back garden; an uncultivated square patch, worn bare in the years when her children played there, and now sprouting a few weeds on its uneven surface. Mitchell, seeing her from the corner of the house, called out her name.

"Oh, it's you again, is it?" was Mrs. Lewis's greeting.

"Yes. Can I have a word with you?"

"Go in and make yourself comfortable," said Mrs. Lewis, "while I finish this lot."

Superintendent Mitchell knew that the front door would be not only locked, but barred, so he walked round to the back and went in. Mrs. Lewis did not bother to look at him as he did so. He made his way to the sitting-room, and, lighting a cigarette, sat down to wait.

The room looked about the same as ever, neither more nor

less prosperous. The Lewises had been through the blitz, though, as usual, Mrs. Lewis had borne the brunt of its effects on their dometisc life. Bert had been away in the Army for part of the time, and after being convicted of stealing from the officers' mess, in prison. Mrs. Lewis had had the house bombed over her head, had been dug out, quite unscathed, and later resettled in the prefab. The children, both very young at the time, had been evacuated to a country hostel some months earlier. So she had emerged from the war with a set of new furniture provided by the government, and here it still was, fairly well cared for and still serviceable. There was also a television set, new since the Superintendent's last visit some three years ago.

When Mrs. Lewis came into the room, drying her arms on her overall, he mentioned this.

"The telly?" Mrs. Lewis gave her usual rich chuckle. "I don't care for it much myself, but they would 'ave it. Glad 'elps with the instalments. She's got a little job, evenings, up at the Corona Cafe. And Reg in the army, that cuts down over'eads. So I manage."

"You always have," said Mitchell.

Mrs. Lewis looked at him, and looked away.

"Seen Bert lately?" he asked.

This was the usual opening, and Mrs. Lewis met it with her usual cheerful calm.

"Wot if I 'ave? I suppose you've come to tell me 'e's in trouble again? Well, is 'e?"

"I don't know," said the Superintendent, truthfully.

"That's something new, and no mistake."

"Has he been here lately?"

"Now and then. You know as well as I do, 'e can't settle. Never did, and never will."

"When was he here last?"

"Why do you want to know?"

"Because he may be in very serious trouble this time."

"It's always serious, isn't it? I've told 'im till I'm blue in the face, 'e'll end 'is days inside if 'e doesn't look out. But this last stretch made an impression on 'im, you can't deny

that. The Welfare Officer says so, too. They even got my
maintenance out of 'im, first job 'e did on discharge. A few
shillings only, but it was a record, I tell you. I was never
more surprised than when it come."

"Mrs. Lewis, when did you last see Bert?"

She looked at him without answering, and he saw an
unusual anxiety in her deep-set, china-blue eyes. He changed
his question.

"Why are you worried about him?"

"'E was different. Mind you, it was the same old Bert in
a way. Full of the wonderful things 'e was doing. The grand
job 'e'd landed for 'isself, real slap-up business, partners, two
of 'em, real class. All the rest of the rigmarole. 'E knows
I don't believe a word of it. Never did, except right at the
start. But that's the way 'is mind works, see. It's all for
'isself, really, 'e goes on that way. Sets 'im up in 'is own
estimation."

"How was he different this time?"

"'E was scared," said Mrs. Lewis, simply.

There was a silence. Then Mitchell said, quietly, "If you
would tell me when this was, I might be able to tell you why
he was scared."

"It was Wednesday, last," she answered, watching him
closely. "'E come along about nine. I was watching the
telly for once, with my neighbour from number eight. Glad
was up at the cafe. We 'eard the knock, and she said, 'You
expecting anyone?' And I thought, 'If that's Bert, after all
these years, and it sounds like 'is knock, she'll think it
peculiar if I wasn't expecting 'im.' So I said, 'Yes. I'm
expecting Bert.' She wasn't 'alf startled. She said, 'I'd best
be going,' and she was out the back door like a cat with a
dog after it, by the time I'd let Bert in the front. 'E said,
'Wot the 'ell is there to laugh at?' So I told 'im, about 'er
going off like that, but it didn't raise a smile, nor a shadow
of one."

"And then?"

"'E come in and 'e set down, and I made to turn off the
telly, but 'e said to let it be, and we just sat 'ere in the dark,

'im that upset 'e was just 'olding on to 'isself, and me wondering, and the damned telly yelling its 'ead off, opera or some such."

"How long did he stay?" asked the Superintendent.

"Only the one night."

"Did he say why he'd come?"

"Does 'e ever? But 'e did say 'e was still going straight. I didn't much like that. It generally means the opposite."

"Do you know where he went from here?"

"No."

"Had he got anything with him?"

"Only 'is overalls, stuffed in the pocket of 'is overcoat, as usual."

"Ah. What was he wearing?"

"'Is suit. Blue serge 'e got when 'e come out last time."

"Doesn't look as if he had been on a job, does it? The overalls, but his suit, not his working clothes."

Mrs. Lewis shook her head.

"I give up trying to make sense out of 'is actions. Give it up years ago. 'E's not normal, you can take my word for that. 'Is 'ead wants examining. They did give 'im a medical once, but it didn't make no difference."

Superintendent Mitchell resisted this mild attempt to switch the conversation.

"Nothing else in his pockets, besides the overalls?"

They exchanged a straight look. There was no concealment in the clear blue eyes.

"I didn't take it on myself to look. I've told 'im, and I've told you, dozens of times, I'm outside of all this. I washed my 'ands of it years back. I've got my own life, see, and my kids' lives to consider. 'E's not my responsibility. There was a time when I thought so, but never no more. I'm not doing no one's dirty work for them, nor I'm not stopping 'em, neether. That's wot I told 'im. 'I'm not asking no questions,' I said, 'but you know as well as I do,' I said, 'they always come to me. So remember that,' I said. But I don't rightly know if 'e took it in, 'e was so damned scared, the poor little beggar."

Mitchell moved to the door.

"Mind if I have a look round?" he asked.

"Please yourself."

It was routine, and they had never before found anything in Mrs. Lewis's house, either the bombed one, or the prefab. But he was as careful and thorough as usual, partly because it was second nature to him, like an experienced doctor examining a heart, but chiefly because of Bert being scared, and having his dungarees rolled up in his overcoat pocket.

So when he felt along the underside of the mattress in Gladys Lewis's bedroom, and came across a flat hard oblong, he had it out in a very few seconds, and found himself looking at a gold cigarette-case, with a monogram on the outside, and no cigarettes within.

He took it to Mrs. Lewis and showed it to her. Her face did not change. She only sighed and said, "I knew it wouldn't last. 'E can't 'elp 'isself. Must be in the blood. It's a disease with 'im. What'll 'e get for that?"

Superintendent Mitchell did not answer at once. He had laid the cigarette-case on the table and stood looking down at it.

"Ever heard of Mr. Oswald Burke?" he said.

Mrs. Lewis was stirred at last. It was clear that she had read all those sensational reports in the daily papers. Her fresh complexion paled.

"Look at that monogram," said Mitchell, relentlessly. "Look at the initials. O.R.B., aren't they? Oswald Reedham Burke."

"No," said Mrs. Lewis, shrinking away from the table. "Not my Bert! You can't pin that sort of thing on my Bert!"

"Where is he, Mrs. Lewis?"

"I've told you I don't know, but if I did, I wouldn't tell you. I never 'ave and I never will. Now you clear out of 'ere, Mister Superintendent Mitchell. You know as well as I do my Bert 'asn't got it in 'im. 'E's more likely to get 'imself done in, than the other way round. You clear out!"

"Just a minute," said Mitchell, putting the cigarette-case

safely away in an inside pocket. "You may like to know that Bert was actually working at the Westminster Gallery the week before the murder was done. And that he, or some-one uncommonly like him, was seen there that Wednesday evening, wearing dungarees, though he'd finished there the Saturday before. And you must have read that a safe was cracked there on Wednesday night. And you can't get out of what you've told me, you know."

Mrs. Lewis broke down and cried, noisily, angrily, acknow-ledging defeat for perhaps the first time in her life. But there was still some fight left in her.

"There's a mistake somewhere," she sobbed. "I'll take my oath, there is. 'E 'asn't got it in 'im, I tell you, and I should know. 'E's treated me as bad as any woman could be, but raise 'is 'and to me, never in 'is life. It isn't in 'im."

Mitchell reflected that many men would think twice before raising a hand to Mrs. Lewis, but he turned away without answering. He was sorry for her. Bert was a bigger fool than he had realized. She had warned him against leaving evidence in her house. He must have known that the police always went to see her as a routine. He had never been quite such a fool before. But he was handicapped by his own twisted nature. The ordinary fence wouldn't look at him; he was too unreliable, too treacherous. Greed had often made him take unsaleable goods, as now. And this time he was afraid. So he had palmed off the evidence of his deed on to his wife. Mean, as usual, and secret, he meant, in some tortuous way, to spread his own guilt to her.

She followed Mitchell to the door of the prefab.

"There'll be nothing of this in the papers, will there?" she asked, huskily. "Nothing to hurt my Glad? She's a good girl. She's doing well. And work! You should just see 'er! It'd go against 'er getting a job if it come out that thing was found in 'er bed. Must that go in? Couldn't it be altered? If my Glad suffers it'll break my 'eart. It will, really."

She began to sob again, and Mitchell felt very uncomfort-able. He wanted to pat her shoulder and assure her that the whereabouts of the gold cigarette-case would never come out, in the Press, at court, or anywhere else. But he pulled himself together.

"It was found inside a mattress," he said. "Which mattress is probably immaterial. The Press will get nothing before we make an arrest."

"You've got to find 'im first," she said, with some return of her usual cheerful acceptance.

"We'll find him," said Mitchell.

Chapter VII

It was a week before they found Bert Lewis, but they did find him, and he was arrested, charged with murder, brought before a magistrate, and remanded in custody.

David Wintringham, who knew the extent and also the limitations of the evidence against Lewis, was not satisfied. The man might have robbed a corpse, must have robbed a corpse, but his whole character and history were against his having committed the major crime in the way it was done.

"You won't get a conviction, Steve," he told the Superintendent. "It was a rash act to arrest him for murder. You'd have done better to keep him as a witness for the real prosecution."

"We collected him in Liverpool," answered Mitchell. "He'd got a passage to South America. On the proceeds from the safe. We were bound to save the expense of getting him back from there, if we ever did."

"What does he say? Anything? Nothing?"

"He talks. He found the cigarette-case in a passage at the Gallery. He made the money for his travelling in a lucky deal last month. He'd come back to the Westminster for his tools, that he'd forgotten when he took his cards the Saturday before."

"Can you break all that down?"

"He never had any tools. Didn't need any for the job he was given. Besides, it was a funny time to go for them *after* working hours, when there'd be none of the men there to tell him where to find them."

"The cigarette-case won't be so easy. It *could* have been dropped anywhere."

"True, but unlikely."

"What about weapons? What was he struck with? Lewis

77

is a little man, isn't he? Couldn't do the trick with the edge
of his hand? "

"No. He must have had a weapon. But there was a good
choice lying about in that place.   There was no blood.
Scarcely any bruise. Any of those metal bars that were all
about could have been used, and as they've been handled a
lot since, it is useless to go over them all for prints. We
have to try, but we won't get anything. He could have left
what he used lying there with perfect safety. Alternatively
he could have taken it out and just across the road and
dropped it in the river."

"All right. Don't get excited, Steve. You've got a long
way to go, and no doubt your little man is where he deserves
to be for snitching the cigarette-case. And a wallet of money,
wasn't there? But I'd take quite long odds he didn't kill.
Jill doesn't think so, either. Nor Tom."

"Tom? "

"Tom Drummond, the artist. The chap who led you to
Bert Lewis."

"Oh, him. Those sketches? Well, I don't know that his
opinion counts for much. I'll give you back that book of his.
We shan't need it now."

Though Superintendent Mitchell was unwilling to give
Tom's drawings the importance they deserved in the development of the case, the young man himself was inclined to see
his own actions in a very different light. Far from being
complacent in the matter, he was profoundly disturbed, and
on that account very angry. Back in London, after a very
unsatisfactory week-end with his family, he stayed indoors
at the studio, moody, remorseful, not attempting to work.
He had never before felt so unsettled.

"Snap out of it, Tom," his friend, Christopher Felton,
urged him. "You've got to answer this bloke's letter. You
haven't even acknowledged his cheque."

"I wish I'd never seen him. I wish I'd never seen any
of them. I wish I hadn't gone to the bloody exhibition that
day."

"Don't be so fatuous. You did go, and you did see them,

and you've got twenty-five quid out of it already, and a commission to paint an oil portrait. That is, if you pull your
socks up and take the commission."

"Blood money."

"Don't be an idiot. This Symington-Cole had nothing
whatever to do with the murder."

"How do you know? He was a friend of Burke's. They
were there together."

"How do you know that? You *saw* them there together.
Did they tell you they *went* there together? Of course not.
They just met there. Besides, friends don't often kill each
other."

"You seem to know a hell of a lot."

As usual, Tom was sitting near the studio window, looking
out over the roofs beyond the railway lines that ran behind
the high wall on the far side of the road. Something in
Chris Felton's voice had broken his concentration upon these
grim roofs and his own disgust. He turned his head to look
at him, automatically transferring his feeling to his friend.
For Christopher's face was lit with a strange amusement.
His voice had been light-hearted enough, but his shining
eyes, his heightened colour, and altogether unsuitable
gaiety, revolted Tom.

"What's up with you?" he asked, heavily. "Been taking
something?"

Felton's face changed. It was true that he occasionally
experimented with this and that to keep up his spirits. And
needed a certain amount of regular stuff, now. He depended
very much on the medicine Hugh Lampton gave him. But
Tom was being unfair, as so often since he met that little
horror, Pauline.

"Why shouldn't I be pleased they've found the—the man
that killed Oswald Burke?"

His voice was petulant now, with a curious undertone of
satisfaction; much more like himself, Tom thought.

"That man could never have killed him."

"Why not?"

The answer was rapped back in something like panic.

"An ordinary labourer? A little chap, half Burke's height? To get behind him and break his neck with that degree of efficiency? Where'd he learn it? Haven't you seen his picture in the papers? I drew him. I know. That's no ex-commando, dislocating necks as easy as birds for the table."

"Don't say things like that!" Chris's voice rose and cracked. "I shall be sick if you say things like that! I shall be sick!"

Tom was furious. The emotional tension in the room had become unbearable.

"Then why start on it? I don't want to discuss the rotten business. Why pick on me first, and then work up the hysterics?"

Felton dropped his face in his hands. He had begun to cry, and he did not want Tom to know it yet.

"If that's all the good your lousy Lampton does you, why go on with him?" Tom persisted. "He's made you ten times worse than you were before."

Chris moaned aloud.

"Pleased this poor bum has been charged with a murder he never did!"

"You don't know he's innocent! I think he did it! I'm sure he did!"

"Oh, no, you're not. You're just scared he may *not* have done it."

The other lifted his racked face and stared at his friend.

"Perhaps *you* did it," Tom said. "Or perhaps you think I did it. Is that it? Do you think I did it?"

He strode to the door, opened it and went out, slamming it behind him.

When his footsteps had died away, Chris Felton got up, tiptoed to the door and opened it. There was not a sound in the house. Felton shut the door again, blew his nose, and went to the telephone.

Though David Wintringham had poured scorn on the police case while he was with the Superintendent, he had to

acknowledge to himself that he had no precise theory to put in its place. He felt it was preposterous to suspect either of the art students. Normal young men, even if they were capable of strong passions, as no doubt Tom Drummond was, did not kill because they were criticized. On the other hand, were they normal young men? He had seen Tom only twice, and Felton only at a distance and not to speak to. He had Jill's report, and he had the strange new drawing of Burke she had found, unmistakably Tom's work, and very disquieting. Tom was certainly excitable. He was also worried about his friend, and that friend's relationship with his psychiatrist. The next move was obvious. See the psychiatrist.

David remembered the man's name. He had no difficulty in finding the telephone number and address, but some trouble in making an appointment. Mr. Lampton's appointment book seemed to be very full. The female voice at the other end was not encouraging. Finally, somewhat to David's surprise, a date and time were fixed, only two days ahead, and at the hour he had himself suggested.

Mr. Lampton lived in a house in Kensington, not far from Gloucester Road. This was off the usual beat for consultants, but then, David reflected, as he sat in the comfortable waiting-room on the ground floor, this man did not seem to be qualified, and he was well placed here, in the middle of minor psychotic country. A host of middle-aged, still well-off people, whose lives had been partially disrupted by war damage and social upheaval, no doubt flocked to receive comfort and encouragement in the release of personal grievances. Having the high priest near at hand with the necessary balm would ensure a regular attendance. And a regular income for Mr. Lampton.

With these unworthy thoughts David occupied the time of waiting. He was alone, and he saw no overcoat, umbrella, gloves, or other sign of a present patient. Not that this necessarily meant there was no patient. He just wondered.

After twenty minutes the receptionist, an elderly woman in a white coat, with the voice David had heard on the telephone, came to fetch him. He was shown into a smaller room at the back of the house and found himself shaking hands with Hugh Lampton.

The man's appearance was exactly suited to his work. He was neither too young nor too old, too formidable nor too insignificant. He looked clever, but not intellectual. In his analysis, David thought, the Greek myths would not obtrude to embarrass the less cultivated or the more modern minds. He had had the impression at the Art Gallery of less height and a less imposing dignity. The former was probably due to seeing him at a distance in the company of Tom and Felton, both tall, and the latter to meeting him on his own ground in his professional surroundings.

These were simple. The inevitable couch, the desk, the armchair, the electric-fire, the shelves of books, the discreet fresh flowers, the soft plain carpet, the soothing colour scheme. All was as it should be. No harsh apparatus was visible, no hard clinical enamel, no glittering chromium instruments, no searching angular lamp at the couch side, no suggestively terrifying white sheet on the couch, no screen. Only a plain upright chair beside a rug-covered divan, to receive the patient's coat and hat, or possibly the psychiatrist himself, taking notes. On the wall above this chair, a charmingly framed small mirror.

"Yes. And not a patient. I hope you got that part of my message."

A little frown appeared on Lampton's forehead and disappeared again at once.

"But about a patient, I presume?"

"No. Not even that. At least, not about a new patient. About one you have already."

With praiseworthy restraint Lampton settled David in the armchair, sat down at the desk himself, and listened. At the end he said, slowly, "You want me to discuss one of my cases with you, because you are engaged unofficially in tracking a murderer, and you have a vague reason to think he may be the man. Isn't that a curious and very unethical request?"

"Possibly," David answered. "On the other hand, as I am so unofficial, I am not primarily dangerous to your patient. And as two medical men——"

"I am a lay psychiatrist," said Lampton, quickly. "Not one of the brotherhood."

David tried another approach.

"I've told you that Tom Drummond is involved, on account of his drawings. He has told me about his friend; I know nothing of young Felton otherwise. Oh, except for what my wife has told me, and seeing him once with you at the Westminster Gallery. So naturally when the question arises how much really did those young men hate Oswald Burke, the answer seemed to be to ask you."

"I see."

For a few seconds Lampton sat, staring down at the blotter on his desk. Then he looked across at David.

"They both hated him like poison," he said, frankly. "I'm not going to say either of them killed him. But I think they hated him enough to wish him dead, and might be prepared to fulfil that wish."

"I've been trying to persuade myself no normal sane young man would think of it seriously for one moment."

"I can't agree with the way you put that. Driven into a frenzy of rage, quite normal sane young men are known to do murder."

"You mean if Burke had been talking to one of them and goaded him with his usual type of criticism?"

"Something like that. Felton is very unstable, I'm afraid. Without going into detail, I should say he might easily lose his head. He has an inflated view of his talent, fostered, alas, by his mother."

"*That* situation!"

"As you say, *that* situation. One doesn't know; one never knows in these cases, which is the real patient, the child or the parent, the wife or the husband. One is asked to treat one, when it should be both." He smiled faintly and David had a sudden conviction that it was at something secret he smiled, not at the words he had just spoken.

"Yes, yes," he answered, deliberately pushing the platitudes on one side. "But I imagine we are not considering Mrs. Felton as a possible murderess?"

Mr. Lampton's eyes glittered with suppressed rage. He was not used to dealing with an intelligence greater than his own. It rattled him.

"Tom Drummond is a powerful young man with very little self-control," he said, sourly. "His grandfather was an ordinary labourer."

"A bricklayer," David corrected. "A skilled craftsman."

"And his father is a self-made man. Peasant stock," persisted Lampton.

"Why not?" said David. "We all are, if you go back the right number of generations."

"You know perfectly well what I mean. Culture, education, prosperous living, all influence the extent and nature of emotional control."

"But the emotions break out just the same. Murderers come from any part of the community. It might be Tom, I agree, but not because his grandfather laid bricks."

"You know perfectly well what I mean," repeated Hugh Lampton, "but you choose to distort it."

There was an adolescent note in his voice that surprised David, but he ignored it and went on.

"In your opinion, then, Drummond has the physique and possibly the primitive urge to murder, but Felton has the psychological twist. Would you say he was definitely psychopathic?"

"Yes, I think I would. His boyhood did not help. He lost his father when he was twelve, and his mother, as I have said, is the doting kind. Also he was ill for several years, with a rather indeterminate abdominal condition. T.B. glands, probably. But his doctors never made up their minds, the X-ray findings were never conclusive. You know how it is."

"Yes," David agreed. "I know how it can be. Mostly symptoms and no signs, I suppose?"

"That's it."

David got up.

"Well, thank you very much," he said. "It was good of you to give me so much of your time."

He drove away from Kensington in a thoughtful mood. When he reached home he looked up Lampton in the Medical Directory, but, though there were a number of examples of that name, none of them was prefixed by Hugh. And yet—and yet—the fellow had not spoken of Felton's early illness in the way a layman would have done. It had been the manner of speaking rather than the words.

"What are you doing?" Jill asked, coming into the room.

"Looking up Lampton."

"I thought he was an unqualified psychiatrist. He isn't there, is he."

"No. That's just it."

"Oh. I see what you mean. Then why not look in an older edition. That one is 1957, isn't it? "

David smiled at her.

"Clever girl," he said. "I never thought of that."

The same evening Tom and Pauline went back to the studio after they left the pub where they always met. There was a biting wind in their faces as they walked up the road, and they were both shivering as they closed the front door of the house.

The studio was deserted, the stove had gone out. Tom was furious.

"Just like Chris to go off without a word of warning and leave the place stone cold," he grumbled. " We were both in all morning. He could have said."

"He never thinks of anything except himself and his miseries," said Pauline, on her knees by the stove. "Chuck me over the matches."

Tom brought them to her and stood watching her get the stove alight, enjoying the sight of her skilful fingers at work.

"I love your hands," he said, gently.

She watched the kindling fire for a few more minutes, then got to her feet and went close to him.

"They're all rough and dirty," she said, turning them over and back. "I don't see anything to rave about."

He took them in his and put them behind his own neck, drawing her closer still.

"I love the way your fingers move," he said. "You *use* your hands. Not like most girls, a bunch of spiked bananas on a thick stalk."

She laughed, stroking the back of his head.

"I'm glad Chris is out," she said. "I wish he always was. Even if I do have to light the stove."

"I know."

He kissed her, but almost at once loosed her hands, and moved away from her to throw himself down on the divan. Pauline made up the fire, which was now well alight, and then went to sit on the floor beside Tom.

"I've taken that commission," he said. "He's giving me a sitting to-morrow. I shan't half feel a fool turning up with the doings in that area."

"Where is it?"

"Welbeck Street. You wouldn't expect Symington-Cole to operate in the back of beyond."

"He might not live there. I thought they shared, umpteen to each house?"

"Not the high-ups like this Cole. At least, that's where he said to come. Two sittings a week for as long as I like."

"How long will it take?"

"God knows. Might never finish it."

"You will. You must! It's the first real portrait you've been asked to make. You know everyone says that's your real line, whether it's academic or not. Who cares, anyhow? You don't, do you? Oh, Tom!" She turned to throw an arm across him. "Tom, darling, you're going to be famous, soon!"

"You make me sick!"

"Why, on earth? Why shouldn't I want success for you?"

"Now then, none of that!"

But he could not suppress his pleasure and his excitement, and for a long time they stayed as they were, before the glowing stove, while, as they talked, their plans for the future rose in more and more splendidly iridescent balloons about their young heads.

Chapter VIII

To m had his first sitting with Symington-Cole the following afternoon. He found it less formidable than he had feared, for the eye surgeon made no attempt to dictate to him how the portrait should be done. Pose, background, and so on, were left entirely to Tom. The portrait was a formal one, he discovered, to be hung in the library of the Medical School at St. Edmund's Hospital. The eye surgeon had not commissioned it personally. It would be paid for from the funds of the learned society that wished so to honour Symington-Cole's outstanding contributions to the surgery of the eye. The sub-committee appointed to find a suitable artist had seen Tom's drawing. Admiration for this, and the thought that a beginner's work would save their pockets, made up for any qualms they felt in engaging an unknown man.

But though the arrangements for the composition of the portrait were left entirely to Tom, he was not satisfied. The well-appointed flat above the surgeon's consulting rooms had no single room in which the lighting was suitable to his purpose. There was only one answer to this. Mr. Cole must give him the next sitting at the studio.

Very reluctantly, thinking of the scruffy state of that house in general, and his own part of it in particular, Tom made his suggestion. To his surprise Symington-Cole agreed at once.

"Naturally," he said. "I expected this. You need that top light, don't you?"

"I'm afraid we have not got a very professional studio. But the light depends partly on the size of the window in relation to the room."

"I'd have thought these were large enough," said Cole,

smiling. "We have to get yards and yards of material when we put up new curtains."

"I can't explain," said Tom, giving up the attempt to do so. "I just know I can't do it in this light."

"All right. Then I'll come to you next time. Do you want to stop now?"

"Oh, no. I'd like to put down a general idea of the surroundings." He smiled, ruefully. "I haven't got anything at all like them at the studio."

Symington-Cole looked at him keenly, but made no answer to this, and the sitting proceeded in silence.

Two days later the eye surgeon went to Mornington Crescent. He appeared to take his new surroundings for granted; he was compliant, took up his pose correctly, held it patiently, did not linger over, or criticize, the crude beginnings of the painting, but merely put down the date of the next visit in his diary. Then he drove away, watched by the landlady, who had spent most of the time of the sitting staring out at the unaccustomed sight of a highly polished Rolls Royce standing at her door.

This sitting took place in the early part of the afternoon. When Symington-Cole had gone away, Tom worked on until the light failed. His morose bad temper had dissolved in the pleasures of dealing with his new problem, and in the purely physical delights of handling paint. He was in a boisterous good mood when Christopher Felton came in. The latter stood in front of the embryo portrait and regarded it gloomily for some time.

"Thomas Drummond, R.A.," he said, at last. There was a spiteful edge to his voice.

"Why not?"

"Chantry Bequest, by the time it's finished."

"Again, why not? Look, Chris, I'm going to make my living this way. I can't afford to do what I like all the time. No professional can. Anyway, I don't dislike this sort of thing."

"Personally," Chris told him, "I'd rather write novelettes for magazines."

"Why don't you, then? You might do it rather well."

They glared at each other. These stupid quarrels kept flaring up, Tom thought, wearily. He suddenly knew he was tired, very tired. And already he was late for his usual meeting with Pauline.

He forced himself to clear up his things properly, clean his brushes, put everything away.

"Are you staying in?" he asked, finally, when he was ready to go.

"I don't know. What the hell has it got to do with you? You don't care, one way or another."

"I don't care for your lousy temper. Your idleness is your own concern. If you are going out, you might make up the stove. It was out the other night."

He got no answer to this, and went away, more than ever fed up with Chris, whose growing neurosis was beginning to reach unsupportable dimensions.

Pauline noticed the smoke the minute they shut the front door behind them. There had been no light in the downstairs rooms as they came up to the house, and there was none under the doors, as they stood in the dark hall. No light anywhere in the house. Only this acrid smell of smoke.

Tom pushed her on one side and went bounding up the stairs. Pauline panted after him. The smoke increased as they mounted.

Tom flung open the studio door. Thick smoke billowed out from a dull red glow, which, as they stared, horrified, turned golden, with a terrible crackling sound.

"Fire alarm!" shouted Tom. "Quick! Run!"

Pauline fled back down the stairs and tore out into the street. She saw several people standing there, pointing upwards, and a figure, farther off, running.

"Fire!" she cried in a shrill voice.

They pointed up the street.

"He's gone to the alarm. Anyone else in there, miss?"

"Yes. Tom."

She was turning to run back into the house, but two men stopped her.

"Better not go back in!"

"I must! I must help him. Let me go!"

She twisted free and disappeared into the hall. One of the two men dashed after her. The other shrugged his shoulders and turned away. If people wanted to commit suicide it was their own lookout.

The man who had followed Pauline caught her up and passed her. The smoke was very thick on the stairs, and the sound of crackling very loud. The leaping flames in the room above grew brighter as they mounted.

"Tom!" screamed Pauline, sick with fear. When she heard his answering shout, her knees gave way and she clung to the banisters, choking and crying.

"You go back in the street!" shouted the man above her. "Don't be a damned nuisance! Go on down!"

He had reached the landing, and found his way barred by canvases, palettes, and other unfamiliar objects. Tom, coughing wildly, his clothes alight, staggered through the doorway. He beat at himself with his hands, and fell against the stair head.

The man tore off his coat, wrapped it round Tom, smothering the flames, and pushed him towards the stairs.

"Down!" he panted. "Get on down!"

But Tom twisted free to snatch up an armful of his precious possessions.

"Bring the canvases," he croaked. "Leave the rest."

Together they bundled the gear downstairs, and emerged into the street just as the fire engine, bell clanging, swung round the corner.

In half an hour the fire was out. The firemen had been able to keep it to the studio, and later the rest of the things Tom had brought out on to the landing were saved, a little scorched and soaking wet, but not irretrievably damaged.

Tom and his helper had carried down five finished pictures
and the unfinished portrait of Symington-Cole. Sitting on
the edge of the pavement on the opposite side of the road,
Tom drew out of his damaged jacket pockets tubes of paint,
pencils, charcoal, and two sketch books.

Pauline, who was kneeling beside him, took these from
him.

"Fancy stopping up there for this lot," she scolded, tears
pouring down her cheeks. "Paint, too. Don't you know it
burns like nobody's business? You'd no right to stay up
there."

"I had to get these." He held out the sketch books to
her. "You take them. Don't let them out of your sight."

Still kneeling beside him, she took them, and stuffed them
into the bucket bag that hung from her arm.

"I thought I might as well get out as much as I could,"
Tom explained. "It wasn't too bad at first. Then the
window burst and that let in a whole lot of air and it all shot
into big flames."

"Oh, Tom, you ought to have left it! You might have
been killed!"

He grinned at her.

"You tried to get back yourself, didn't you? I heard that
chap yelling at you to go down."

"Of course I had to. You were up there."

He took her hand, and she saw the spasm of pain that
crossed his face.

"You're hurt!"

"Nothing much. I got alight at one stage. Had to try
to put it out. The chap who came up saved me."

He nodded towards the man who stood talking to one of
the firemen. He was still in his shirt sleeves, grimy, dis-
hevelled, and as matter of fact as ever.

"Give him back his coat," Tom said. The pain in his
hands was worse now. He was afraid he might faint.

While Pauline hesitated, the man looked round, and seeing
Tom struggling to free himself from the coat, came over to
him.

"No, son. You keep it on till the ambulance comes. It'll be here any minute now."

"Fuss," Tom muttered, but no one took any notice.

Before the ambulance took him away, Pauline had thought of a plan of action, and Tom approved it. She would ring up the Wintringhams, explain the situation, and ask if she might place the sketch books in David's care. She would take the rest of the things to her own lodging.

In the end she did not have to carry out the second part of her plan. The fire had gutted the studio, but the two small bedrooms on the same floor were unharmed. They could still be used, at any rate as a store for the rescued canvases.

Pauline was thankful to find that Tom had not lost all his clothes, such as they were. Nor Chris Felton, either. She was not allowed to go back into the house, but the policeman in charge took the key of Tom's bedroom, which he had given her, and promised that the odd collection on the pavement would be taken care of.

She did not tell them about the sketch books. When she had given her meagre account of how they had found the studio on fire, and her part in what followed, she was allowed to go. She saw a cruising taxi as she reached the main road, hailed it, rather surprised at her own extravagance, and was carried off to Hampstead.

Tom Drummond spent two days in hospital, being treated for shock and slight burns on both hands. Everyone told him he had been very lucky. Some told him also that he had been a fool. He did not agree with this, but was not inclined to argue. What interested him more, and puzzled him a great deal, was how and why the fire had started.

Chris said it must have been the stove. He had done as Tom asked him, he said, and filled it up, leaving it partially open, to keep it drawing. He might have overdone this, and it had got too hot, he said. Then there was some evidence that a canvas had fallen against it. If the stove was overheated, this canvas might have started to smoulder, and then its inflammable paint would begin to burn.

The explanation was glib, and altogether too easy, Tom thought. Not in the least convincing. But it seemed to be the one accepted, and as far as he knew Chris was not being blamed by the authorities for carelessness, either in over-stoking the stove, or in leaving an inflammable object near it, so insecurely propped up that the vibration of a passing lorry could make it topple over.

Chris was, however, being blamed by the landlady, who had come home from the pictures with her husband to find a crowd still gathered about her house, and the house itself full of water and large firemen, wearing asbestos gloves, and carrying little axes. As soon as the pair had recovered from their initial shock, they had sought at once to lay the blame. The consequence of this was a demand for damages, and a request to leave immediately.

Tom did not altogether regret this outcome. It had been only a question of time. Chris Felton had become impossible to live with, and though Tom could not help feeling it was partly his fault, the basic trouble, he knew, had nothing to do with him. He visited Tom in hospital on the day after the fire; to explain the landlady's ultimatum, and to say that he had already arranged to go to Hugh Lampton, who would put him up until he found himself another studio. He was not going to his mother's flat, he told Tom. It was a grand, a unique opportunity to prove his independence.

"Which is all very well," said Pauline, when she heard Tom's account of all this the next day, after he had left the hospital. "But he depends on her for every penny, doesn't he?"

"You bet."

They were sitting on the side of Tom's bed at the lodgings in Mornington Crescent. There was still a sharp smell of old bonfires in the air of the room. The studio door was boarded up. All that had been salvaged from it, either during the fire or afterwards, was stacked against the bedroom wall.

"Oh, well," said Tom. "Let it go. Chris has, already."

"Is that my fault at all?" Pauline asked, demurely. She sincerely hoped it was, but she was not quite sure what Tom thought.

He pulled her into his arms.

"Yes. Of course it is, thank God."

After a time they went on with the packing. Tom had to move his possessions that day, the landlady insisted. Fortunately he had arranged where to go, or rather Pauline had arranged it for him. Until he found himself another studio the Wintringhams had offered to let him have one of the top rooms in their house. It had no skylight, but it faced north-east, and the window was large, with a marvellous view over the Heath, Pauline told him. It had been used as a box-room, but the Wintringhams were moving out the trunks and suitcases to a smaller room, and sorting out a few pieces of furniture to put in it. They had a camp bed he could use.

"Mrs. Wintringham said to go there any time we were ready," Pauline said, packing away the last of Tom's shirts.

"The sooner the better. Lucky I've got the rent handy to settle up with the old bitch downstairs."

Pauline did not remind him that this was also due to the kindness of the Wintringhams. She was afraid, if she did, he might refuse to stay in their house, and she was anxious that he should go there. Because Dr. Wintringham had been very pleased with her for bringing him the sketch books on the night of the fire, and she had heard him say to his wife, "Keeps turning up, doesn't it? I wish I hadn't given it back to him. Perhaps it was meant to be destroyed this way. What do you think?" Pauline wanted to find out exactly what he had meant by this.

However, life for Tom in Hampstead settled down into a fresh routine of work. Symington-Cole continued the sittings twice a week, and during the first fortnight of Tom's stay in the Wintringhams' house the portrait made good progress.

Or so Tom said, but he kept it covered and would not show it to anyone, not even the subject, himself.

Pauline noticed this new, secretive mood at once, and with misgiving. The rescued canvases, she found, were tied together and stacked in a corner of the room. When she suggested spreading them out, to clean them and to see if there was any serious damage, Tom snapped at her to leave them alone and mind her own business.

"Why?" she asked, too much surprised to take offence.

"Because I say so. I don't want everyone looking at my things."

"Meaning me, or the Wintringhams? But they like your work, Tom. Or Nanny? I don't think she'd be interested. She never comes up here, does she?"

"Not when I'm in."

"*She* isn't a snooper. She'd be horrified at the bare idea. She's a real Edwardian relic."

"She's all right," said Tom, unexpectedly. He was thinking of his first day at Hampstead, when he had been grumbling about the necessity of going to the hospital to have the dressings on his hands changed.

"Are they bad?" she had asked him. And when he said no, only sore where the blisters had been, she had taken him off into the kitchen, and fetched a box of penicillin tulle and bandaged him up as skilfully and much more securely than the little probationer in the out-patient department of the hospital. Since then he had gone to her every morning after breakfast, and one hand was completely healed and the other one nearly so.

"If you aren't afraid of Nanny looking at your things," insisted Pauline, "and I don't see what harm she could do if she did, what is there to worry about?"

But Tom would not tell her. He simply led her away from the pile of canvases standing against the wall, and told her to get ready, because they were going out.

So the two weeks passed. And then one day, when Pauline arrived at the Wintringhams' house, she found Tom was out.

"But do go up and wait for him in his room if you want to," said Jill, who had let her in.

"May I, really?"

"Of course."

Pauline climbed the stairs, thinking how pleasant life was when people did not suspect your motives and therefore try to get rid of you; or, on the other hand, feel obliged to entertain you, making a wholly unwanted fuss. Jill Wintringham simply spoke to her kindly and took her for granted.

Pauline reached the room on the top floor and sat down, out of breath from climbing the stairs. She was facing the stack of canvases as she sat; her curiosity was unappeased; Tom was not there. She went to them, untied the string, and turned them round, one by one.

There was a remarkable change in Tom's pictures. They had been a varied collection; one or two landscapes, developed from his early efforts; one or two portraits, with herself as model; an unfinished painting of Christopher Felton; a still life; a scarcely begun self-portrait. The usual exercises in technique of the very young beginner, but all showing the unmistakable mark of his talent. She remembered them all, and yet the changes, which he must have made during the last two weeks, were astonishing.

Into the foreground of the landscapes figures had been painted; very sinister figures, that stood out, dominating the scene, and gathering it into their own being. This was strange enough, but the most disturbing thing of all was that these figures, and Christopher, and herself, and even his own face, so lightly indicated in the self-portrait, bore the same expression, and gazed abroad from the same eyes, hard, piercing, impersonal, cruel. The eyes he had given to Oswald Burke in his later sketch of him. The eyes of the critic, whom he had loathed.

Quickly she turned the pictures away, with their faces to the wall. Something was very wrong here. Something had happened to Tom. Was it the result of the fire, or had he already, before that, begun to alter his paintings? With a sudden chill at her heart, she remembered the drawing Jill

G

had found under the cushion in the old studio. The eyes
again, and that time in yet another rendering of Oswald
Burke.

She decided to go down at once to Mrs. Wintringham and
tell her what she had found. But as she was moving across
the room to the door, it opened, and there was Tom, looking
at her with soft eyes and smiling.

" Hullo, darling," he said. " I see you've beaten me to it."

Chapter IX

THE case of Bert Lewis, charged with the murder of Oswald Burke, went through the magistrate's court. He was committed for trial at the Old Bailey.

Superintendent Mitchell was satisfied that he had a case, and one that followed a known pattern. The habitual thief, surprised in the act, determined to avoid yet another sentence, had resorted to violence. He might not have intended to kill, merely to have rendered the interrupter incapable of betraying him. But he had killed, and as things now stood, he might be found guilty of capital murder.

David Wintringham, on the other hand, was far from satisfied. The official solution was straightforward, but it was far too simple. General rules should not be applied to human conduct, except very roughly. Certainly not in a case surrounded by so many complex and subtle relationships. To assume the guilt of Bert Lewis, a total stranger, was to ignore the several hatreds directed at Oswald Burke, of which he, David, had proof. It was to ignore, as well, the suggestion carried by Tom Drummond's sketch book; the torn out pages, the duplicated portraits, the attempt, surely deliberate, to destroy the book altogether.

For no reasonable explanation had emerged to account for the fire at the artists' studio. On the contrary. The firemen had reported several suspicious circumstances that seemed to suggest it might have been arranged. It was strange that everyone living in the house was out at the time, and possibly stranger still that Tom and Pauline arrived back, unusually early for them, and just in time to discover it before it really got hold. True, Tom seemed to be concerned, very much concerned, to save his own property. Had he been equally careful to see that Christopher Felton's few paintings, his considerable number of books and photographs, had been lost?

When David reviewed the case with Jill, they both decided that the only way to get fresh light on it was to go back to the beginning.

"The answer is, of course, in the Art Gallery," said David. "Not now, I mean. It was there, the whole answer, on the evening of that Wednesday."

"And we were there, too," said Jill. "Only we didn't see anything important."

"Oh, yes, we did. We saw Tom's drawings, and those are all-important, I think."

"What I mean is, we didn't see anything sinister or signifi-cant. Even Lampton, who surely is rather a dark horse, was only standing with Chris Felton at the other side of a public room. If we'd met him creeping about the downstairs part of the Gallery, or hiding behind a pillar——"

"Don't be frivolous."

"Well, you know what I mean."

"Of course I do. And you're quite right. We have noth-ing to offer Steve. Nor has Tom, or says he hasn't. Apart from that unfortunate drawing of Bert Lewis, which has mucked up the whole business as far as Scotland Yard is concerned. It would be useless to expect to get anything out of Felton. He'd never say a word that he thought might incriminate his idol, Lampton. He'd only tell him where our thoughts are wandering. If only Steve wasn't so sold on the Lewis build-up."

"Steve is a professional policeman," sighed Jill. "You can't expect him to do anything else. The stupid little man kept Burke's cigarette-case, and that damns him completely."

"It does not prove that he murdered Burke."

They were back where they had started, and both fell silent. At length Jill said, "Obviously, we must find some-one else who was in the Westminster that afternoon, and noticed something odd. The only *people* we know were there are the ones in Tom's book. And the only named ones——"

"The only named ones we haven't tried, or decided not to try, are those television stars. What was the name? "

"I don't remember. But you can ask Steve."

"And I will."

So, the next day being his free afternoon, David drove to Lime Grove and plunged into that factory of mechanized entertainment.

It took some time to establish what he wanted at the reception desk. But after a time a messenger boy came and was told to take him up. This meant a long ascent in a lift, and a still longer walk down a narrow passage lined with doors, like a large hotel. There were no windows, and the air was warm and stuffy. Most of the doors were shut, but a few were open, and through them David caught glimpses of girls in various costumes, modern, historical, music hall chorus, or ballet. Also of a few men, mostly in checked shirts without jackets, holding scripts, and talking volubly.

The messenger unlocked a door, handed the key to David, and invited him to go in.

There was no one there. The air inside was as stuffy as that in the corridor, and far hotter. The room, which was only a narrow cell, had two chairs, some hooks for clothes on the wall, and a long mirror.

The boy shut the door and vanished. David sat down to consider the next move. From what he had seen as he came along he decided that this was a dressing-room, and that he had been taken for a performer. Probably in the show that starred the Ellis pair. He had repeated their names many times at the reception desk, in trying to make his mission clear. Evidently the names alone had got through. However, he seemed to be in the right territory, though with a false identity. As nothing happened for the next ten minutes, he decided to go out and reconnoitre.

Another few minutes passed. None of the characters he saw moving about or standing in corners or sitting inside open doors, took any notice of him at all. At last he stopped a young man, more formally dressed than the others, who was leaning against the wall, polishing horn-rimmed spectacles and deep in thought.

"I am looking for Cyril and Lily Ellis," said David, simplifying his purpose to the bare essentials.

"Number Three," said the young man, not looking up from his work on his glasses.

"I beg your pardon?"

This aroused a faint interest. The young man came off the wall and put on the glasses.

"Studio Three. Know where that is?"

"No."

A messenger boy was passing. The young man caught him.

"Jimmy," he said. "Can you take this gentleman to Number Three?"

"O.K., Mr. Rice."

David followed again. This time they emerged from the warren of dressing-rooms into a larger space with more lifts. Another brief ascent brought them to the studio.

"Mind the cables," whispered the messenger, and promptly disappeared.

David moved through a wide opening into a vast barn, in darkness, except for a concentration of light upon one small section. Here a backcloth showed a very luscious, full-blown, midsummer garden, before it stood an extremely knobbly rustic bench, and on the bench an amply-built young woman, in a wide straw hat and fichu, sat with eyes upturned to an elegant, frock-coated, breeched and generously chested young man. They were both singing their heads off. David thought he had never before heard, at such close quarters, so much vibrating sentiment.

A group of men and women stood between him and this palpitating scene. They stared, not at the performers, but at the monitor set, where the figures appeared in black and white, the garden losing its glowing colour, the singers curiously reduced in impact, as in size.

The song came to an end, other lights came on, the singers

relaxed and began chatting to one another, while technicians rushed about, and the producer and director conferred heatedly with their backs to the crowd.

Almost at once, beyond the group where he stood, David saw the cameras begin to move on to the next set, their long thick cables trailing and twisting behind them. Far off, inside their glass-walled cage, the manipulators of the final offering got up and stretched and came forward to peer down into the studio.

"Can you tell me," David asked quietly of the man nearest to him, "where I can find Cyril and Lily Ellis?"

The man stared at him. Then he repeated slowly, as if to a child, "Did you say the Ellises?"

"Yes."

"You've just seen them." His voice was faint with astonishment.

"You mean—the two in that—er—garden, who have just been singing?"

"Yes."

"I'm sorry," said David. "I didn't know they sang."

"You didn't know——"

"I haven't got television," said David, losing patience, "so there is no reason why I should know, is there?"

The man turned away from him, obviously anxious to escape from a proved madman who might do him a mischief at any moment. David's short laugh only made him turn startled eyes, and hurry on.

The Ellis pair were leaving the set now, having finished their part in the rehearsal. They were moving in his direction, so David stepped forward in their path.

"You won't know who I am," he said. "But my name is Wintringham. I wonder if I might speak to you both for a minute about something not in the least connected with television."

The stars exchanged glances. The girl nodded. All three moved away from the group of producers, directors and technicians into a far corner of the big barn-like studio. David explained his purpose.

" I don't know if Scotland Yard contacted you earlier? " he asked, at the end.

" Well, yes," Cyril Ellis answered. " Just to ask if we'd noticed this man Bert Lewis when we were at the Art Gallery."

" Had you? "

" No."

" Did Superintendent Mitchell tell you how he knew you were there? "

They smiled, the innocent confident smile of popular favourites.

" We can't help it," the girl said. " We don't go out of our way to get it."

She meant publicity, and David tactfully left it at that, except to explain again that he, personally, had not had the pleasure before that day——

" Then how did you know? If the Yard didn't tell you? "

" I'll show you," said David, opening Tom's book of drawings.

The Ellises were delighted. They wanted to know who Tom was, where he could be found. They wanted to buy their picture there and then. It was with difficulty that David got them to concentrate on the other drawings.

" Never mind about Bert Lewis, now," he said. " Look through them slowly and if you recognize anyone you saw that afternoon tell me."

" After all these weeks? "

" I know it's an outside chance. But try."

They bent their heads over the book.

" That's one," said Lily.

" No, it isn't. That's Burke, the chap that was murdered. You've been seeing enough of him in the papers to recognize him here. That's right, isn't it? " Cyril asked, turning the book round.

" Yes."

" There's Lewis, the murderer! This boy is wonderful at a likeness, isn't he? "

" Lewis is not convicted yet," murmured David.

"Didn't he do it, then? Trust the police to make a hash of it."

"They are very often right. And very painstaking in any case."

"You've said it," murmured Lily, regretfully.

"Now there," said Cyril, stopping and appealing to her. "Isn't that the chap we saw on the embankment?"

"The one I said looked as if he was throwing up into the river? Let me see."

She bent over the sketch, and nodded.

"It's very like. He turned round as we passed, and gave me such a look."

"Your voice carries, dear."

"I only asked you was he ill, and said people oughtn't to be sick into the Thames."

"Yes. And when we'd passed, I told you I'd just seen him in the toilet at the Gallery."

"What time was that?" David asked, quickly.

"Oh, I don't know, I'm sure. Lateish. Just before closing time. We didn't get there till late. But we'd had enough, hadn't we, Lil?"

"That's right. We were told we ought to go, but I can't say I got much out of it, myself. Anyway, the attendants were starting to clear the people out when we left."

"And this man was outside by then?"

"That's right," answered Cyril. "He left the toilet before I did."

"I think he was waiting for someone to come out of the Gallery," said Lily. "I looked back once or twice as we walked away. We'd parked the car in that side road. And he left the embankment, this man did, and crossed the road, and stood at the bottom of the Gallery steps, looking up. I thought, then, he must be a bit cracked, and not sick, after all."

"Well," said David. "Thanks very much. I'm most obliged to you both."

He took the sketch book away from them. They looked disappointed.

"Aren't you going to tell us what all this is in aid of?"
Cyril asked.

"Sorry. Not at present. But I'm very grateful. If anything comes of it, I'll certainly get in touch. And if you
want to contact the artist about your picture, write to him
care of me."

He wrote on an envelope.

"There you are. Names and address."

With that the two singers had to be content.

When he reached home that evening, David found Jill
writing letters. She stopped as he came in.

"Carry on," he said, deliberately casual.

"You know I can't, till I know what happened at Lime
Grove."

He told her.

"It isn't very helpful, is it?" she asked. "We know from
Tom that Lampton and Chris were still at the Gallery when
he left."

"This was Lampton by himself."

"Waiting for someone—or something?"

"Apparently."

"Do you think Chris was still inside?"

"Could be. But the place was being closed at that time."

"Did you ask Lampton about leaving? I mean, whether
he was with Chris or by himself, and about the time?"

"No. There did not seem to be any point then, and I
didn't want to scare him. My inquiries were about Tom,
chiefly. It seemed the best lead, and got us on to Chris, as I
meant it to."

"I see. So this afternoon was a washout?"

"Not entirely. We have some idea of Lampton's movements from independent witnesses. If he gives a different
account himself, we can work on that."

"You mean, if he wanted to shield Chris——"

"Or himself."

"Why Lampton? What possible connection? Oh, of
course. There is something odd about him. But he wasn't
in the medical directory, was he?"

"He was not. Neither my recent copy, nor the older ones at St. Edmund's. But it was something quite different I discovered this afternoon. I'll show you."

He turned the pages of the sketch book until he found a drawing of a woman. It was a head and shoulders: a dowdy hat sat on untidy hair, above a very ordinary face. Below, a few lines suggested a loose overcoat, and beneath it a plain blouse with a brooch at the neck.

"Remind you of anyone?" David asked.

"Yes. Vaguely."

She turned the pages, searching.

"You won't find it," David told her. "It was torn out."

"Oswald Burke!"

"Exactly. The first one of Burke that Tom showed us at the Gallery, and which he afterwards destroyed, or Chris did, we don't know for certain. She's the dead spit of Burke as he was when James introduced us to him. Can't think why I didn't notice it before, except that the other drawing was gone."

"We didn't notice it when we were looking through at the Gallery, did we?"

"It wasn't there, then."

"Oh, don't be mysterious. Explain."

"You see," said David, turning the pages slowly. "It comes just before Bert Lewis, and after the girls looking at Dame Ellen. That suggests Tom did it in the hall of the Gallery, very shortly before he left himself, doesn't it?"

"Yes. Which was after we'd gone, so we didn't see it."

"Correct."

"Who is she?"

"That's what I want to know. But she may not really be like Burke at all."

"Oh! Why?"

"Because," said David, "you know as well as I do that Tom is obsessed by his idea of Burke. He could have given just that twist to any commonplace woman's features, to turn her into another Burke."

"Yes, he did. Not when he drew him first, but after **we** told him. Which is when that sketch was made."

They sat looking at the drawing for some seconds. Then Jill said, "Have you seen his recent work at all? What he's been doing since the murder?"

"I thought he was painting James."

"So did I. So did Pauline. She was worried, so she had a look, and next day she came to me. They've gone out, just now. Do you think we could go up to his room for you to see, too?"

"Almost anything is allowed in this game. After all, murder is not allowed, is it?"

They looked at all the canvases, and they looked at the unfinished portrait of Symington-Cole. His lean, ascetic face was less frightening than the imagined ones that had appeared on the other paintings.

"Tom seems to be keeping to the job here, at any rate," said David. "Rather too much so, by the looks of it. For him, this work is on the dull side. I don't think his heart is in it, any more. Perhaps it never was."

"What about the others?"

"I think," said David, slowly, "this murder may be the making of him. He has begun to paint his ideas and his experience, and he has stopped, I imagine for ever, being a good little photographer. You can't go back on that sort of thing."

"But *what* experience?" Jill insisted. "I agree Burke is now a symbol. But a symbol of what? Evil? Violence? Horror? Mortality? *Or his own guilt?*"

"We shall have to find out, shan't we?" said David, gravely.

Chapter X

TOM DRUMMOND was beginning to have a conscience about his friend Christopher. He had not seen him more than once in the three weeks he had been living in Kensington with Hugh Lampton. This had been for a short conversation at the usual pub, where he was waiting for Pauline. He was surprised and touched that Chris had taken the trouble to come all that way to see him, and they talked with more ease than for a long time. But as soon as Pauline arrived, Chris went away. That had been quite ten days ago, and Tom was beginning to feel guilty. He should have followed his friend's lead, and made a visit to him in turn.

"You'll have to go and look him up at his own place," Pauline said, reasonably. "You know he can't stand the sight of me."

"It isn't all that easy," Tom answered. "It isn't his place, for a start. It's that stinker, Lampton's."

"Go when Lampton isn't there."

"How do I find that out? He's always there. He works, as he calls it, in that house."

"Ring up Chris and find out when you can go. He knows you don't want to meet Lampton. He wouldn't want you to meet him, now. You destroy his illusions about the witch doctor."

"Too right. I suppose I could try."

Chris Felton did not sound at all happy, Tom thought, when he spoke to him on the telephone. But he was willing to see Tom, even eager, and suggested the following Saturday when Hugh Lampton was going to be away for the week-end. He suggested a time between four and six, explaining that his treatment now included a long rest, lying down, in the afternoon.

"With dope, I don't mind betting," Tom said, bitterly, to Pauline, after he had rung off. "I wish to God I could break up that combination."

She looked at him curiously.

"Why? Are you so fond of Chris? Or do you just hate Hugh? I don't get it."

"I'm sorry for him. Chris, not the trick cyclist. He's in a trap, caught between his frightful mother and that phoney soul-mixer."

Pauline laughed.

"He's certainly mixed up Chris good and proper," she said. "Let's go."

On Saturday afternoon they went for a stroll in Hyde Park and Kensington Gardens. Pauline was impatient to get Tom's visit over.

"O.K.," he said. "Where shall we meet, after?"

"I'm coming with you."

"I'm damned if you are!"

"I'm coming to the door. If Chris has changed his mind, I'll be there to stop you losing your head and acting silly."

He gave her a great hug, to the indignation of an elderly woman with a small dog, which was startled by the action, and let out shrieks of alarm.

"O.K., Girl Guide," he said. "But you can't hang around the doorstep."

"I'll sit in the hall. When you've had your talk, and settled your conscience, and Chris throws you out, we'll go to the pictures."

Lampton's house appeared to be deserted. They rang the bell several times, and were on the point of going away, when a woman appeared in the area and called up to them to know what they wanted.

"We were told to call," Tom said, cautiously.

"Mr. Lampton has gone away for the week-end. Went last night."

"We've come to see Mr. Felton."

"Oh, him!"

The woman stood, hesitating, looking up at them.

"He is in, isn't he?" Pauline asked, annoyed by her manner.

"I couldn't say, I'm sure. He usually rests in the afternoon, but to-day I heard him pacing up and down for hours. I think he's lying down, now. Not heard a sound the last quarter hour. But you never know if he's in or out, except when his mother calls. You can't help knowing he's in, then."

"Mrs. Felton is not here now, is she?"

"Not that I know of." The woman appeared to be relenting, for she went on, "You friends of his?"

"Old friends," said Tom, firmly. "He and I used to share a studio. Then we had a fire."

She nodded.

"I heard that was why he come here. Another artist, are you? Oh, well, I'd better let you in, I suppose?"

"Giving us a big welcome, isn't she?" said Pauline, as they stood on the steps again outside the front door.

"Shut up! She's coming."

The door opened, and they were shown inside. The woman, who seemed to be the caretaker, and in fact combined that office with those of housekeeper and receptionist, asked them if they knew their way, and without waiting for an answer, went on, "Second floor, door opposite you. That's his bedroom."

Tom walked upstairs, the caretaker retired to the basement, and Pauline, as arranged, sat down on a hall chair.

But not for long. In a very short time Tom appeared at the bend of the stairs.

"Come up!" he said, in an urgent whisper. "Quickly!"

She ran up at once, following him through an open door into a bedroom. Christopher Felton lay on the bed, apparently asleep. His face was flushed, with a blueish look about his lips. He was breathing slowly and heavily.

"I can't rouse him," Tom said.

Pauline tried to waken the sleeper, but also failed.

"Must have taken an overdose," she said, when she stopped, panting. "Get a doctor!"

Tom did not need prompting. The housekeeper, hearing the commotion, came up from her basement, and did her best to hinder his efforts with her own excited suggestions. But he paid no attention to her orders, protests and abuse. In a short time a doctor was found. Within half an hour Chris was in hospital.

"Lucky for him you turned up when you did," David Wintringham said.

Tom and Pauline were back in Hampstead.

"Damned lucky. Luckier still he was disturbed, thinking of me going there, and put off his rest beyond his usual time. I think he did that on purpose, so that I'd find him asleep and go away. He's like that, sometimes. They say he has a chance, but if we'd found him a couple of hours later it would have been too late."

"When were you meant to arrive?"

"Between four and six. Actually I said I might be late, but wouldn't be early."

"Were you late?"

"No. As a matter of fact, I was early. Very early, weren't we, Pauline?"

She nodded.

"My fault," she said. "I didn't see why we should muck up the second part of the afternoon, breaking into it to see Chris. So I said if we went about three he'd have had time for this rest, and we could get away before four."

"And that was what you did?"

"That's right."

Tom looked very miserable.

"If the poor blighter wanted to finish it," he said, "I've scrubbed that out for him, haven't I?"

"Do you honestly think he was attempting suicide?"

"I don't know."

There was an artificial note in Tom's voice that caught David's attention.

"You do think he might. Then why? Because he knows something about Burke's murder? Or about Lampton?"

"Are you suggesting *Lampton* had anything to do with Burke's death?" Tom asked, eagerly.

"I'm just wondering."

David was also wondering why Tom had seized upon his second question and ignored the first. Did he, perhaps, know something harmful to Chris, or did he merely fear what the unstable boy might have done?

"Anyway," he said, to change the subject. "You've nothing to reproach yourself with, Tom. On the contrary."

Later that evening, discussing the new development with Jill, David said, "It doesn't sound quite right for suicide, you know. Felton could easily have put Tom off, if he wanted to make a job of it. Putting off the time of his rest would work the opposite way."

"Perhaps he only wanted to make an exhibition of himself. And took good care not to fall into danger."

"But he didn't. If Tom had kept to the stated time, it would have been too late."

"That's the opposite of what you've been saying. Perhaps the poor boy couldn't make up his mind. He would, and then he wouldn't. Finally he made up his mind and swallowed the pills."

"Yes. That's in character. But you'd think in that case he'd hesitate over the dose as well. Hysterics usually arrange for their own safety. But he had taken a lethal dose. They seem to have washed out more than enough to kill him."

"If it wasn't suicide, then someone planted those pills for him to take. Would that be Lampton? But *why* would Lampton want to kill Chris? Isn't he, or rather, his mother, the goose that lays the golden eggs?"

"Yes, she is. I don't know why."

"If it is anything to do with Burke's murder, why wait till now, when Chris is living in his own house, and suspicion must fall on him? Surely it would have been easier at the studio in Mornington Crescent?"

"Ah! The studio. That little fire was started deliberately, Steve tells me."

H

"They've proved it, have they? Well, was it to burn Chris?"

"Oh, no. He was out. Everyone was out. To burn Tom's sketch book, I think."

"But why not just take it and burn it in that stove they had?"

"That would be too obvious. Burning the studio was meant to look like an accident."

"How silly, when the firemen and the police saw at once that it was not!"

"Very silly, but criminals are like that. Cunning, ingenious, but never able to think that other people may know more than they do."

"Besides, anyone who knows Tom knows that he can always draw his people again from memory. He drew another Oswald Burke, didn't he?"

"He couldn't draw *all* the people again. He would remember the ones he knew or got to know. He would not remember the casuals, the staff, the passers-by we are not interested in. But there may be one among those that Lampton or Chris Felton do not want identified."

"Such as that woman with a face like Burke's. You keep harping on Lampton, now. Is there any possible motive for him? Oh, I know he hated Burke for trying to interfere with his treatment of Chris. But he has Mrs. Felton on his side, and she pays. So Burke was really quite powerless, wasn't he? Surely Lampton had no valid motive for murder?"

"Not over Chris, no. But suppose Burke knew something about Lampton, and was trying to loosen his hold on Chris by blackmail. What then?"

"That sounds terribly melodramatic! I don't believe Oswald Burke would ever think of doing such a thing."

"I don't mean blackmail for money. Simply a demand to leave Chris to his mother, and get the hell out."

"I still don't believe that kind, sensible man would do it."

"You are thinking of the Burke we talked to, aren't you? What about this Burke?"

He unlocked his brief case and took out the sketch book.

"Is that where it lives now?" said Jill, smiling.

"It is. For as long as I can keep Steve from asking for it back. He has kept the Bert Lewis drawing, and he believes still that it is the only one he's interested in."

"Good luck to him!"

"What about *this* Burke?" David repeated.

Jill looked at the drawing that Tom had done after he knew the critic's identity, when Burke was looking at a sculpture.

"Yes," she said, with a little shiver. "A different being altogether. Almost as bad as the ones Tom has done since. And that is authentic, isn't it? It was done before the murder. Was he like that in ordinary life, or only when he was on the job?"

"Who can say?"

Jill thought this over. Then she said, "I think I know someone who could tell us. And about some other things too. Mrs. Felton."

"Go and ask her, then."

"Do you think I could?"

"I don't see why not."

Thinking it over, later on, Jill Wintringham could see quite a number of reasons for not attempting to pump Mrs. Felton. In the first place there was their earlier meeting at the studio. It had been far from cordial. Mrs. Felton had not liked her, and she had found Mrs. Felton deplorable. On the other hand, Chris Felton's present condition, still serious, had probably softened her, and must have changed her view of Tom Drummond. Since Tom was now a part of the Wintringham household, Mrs. Felton might think more kindly of David and herself.

This very faulty logic comforted Jill as she sat at the hospital, where she had gone to reconnoitre the position, and take flowers to Chris, who had recovered consciousness, and was out of immediate danger.

"No visitors, I'm afraid," the nurse said, accepting the flowers.

"I didn't expect to see him," Jill answered.

"His mother is here," the nurse went on, trying to be helpful. "Would you like to have a word with her? She's in Sister's room. Now he is conscious, we don't let her sit in the cubicle all the time."

Jill smiled, and seeing it, the nurse allowed herself to laugh gently.

"She's been terribly upset, poor dear," she said, recovering her proper gravity. "He isn't very kind to her, I think, and she's so devoted. He doesn't speak to her as a son should speak to his mother."

Jill nodded, and followed her to Sister's room. Mrs. Felton was indeed a spectacle of grief, almost of despair. The bright self-confidence, the brash arrogance, were gone. An unhappy, anxious woman confronted Jill, too much absorbed in her own trouble to remember her former impression of her.

"It's good of you to inquire," she said, when she understood who Jill was. "I'd like you to tell Tom how grateful I am. I couldn't bear to see him yet, but I am truly grateful."

"I'll tell him," Jill promised.

They talked for a few minutes. Mrs. Felton was evidently quite convinced that Chris had tried to take his own life.

"I don't know what to do with him now," she said, rather as if Chris were a pet dog that had turned nasty. "They say he will be quite well in a few days. But he won't, will he? He must be mentally ill, much worse than I thought, to do a thing like that."

"It doesn't look as if Mr. Lampton's treatment had been particularly successful," suggested Jill. At last she had been able to bring in the psychiatrist's name. But if she expected an outburst from Mrs. Felton, she was disappointed.

"Poor Hugh," said the widow, sadly. "He never seems to succeed, somehow." She hastened to add, "Though a lot of his patients think very highly of him."

"Do they?"

"Oh, yes, indeed. So, considering his great handicap——"

"*Handicap!*" exclaimed Jill, finding this word astonishing in such a context.

"Perhaps I ought not to have said that. But Hugh Lampton has not had an easy time. Some woman, I believe—an unfortunate and damaging case—but I mustn't say a word."

"Of course not," agreed Jill, wondering how to further Mrs. Felton's already considerable indiscretion.

"I don't know much in any case," said Chris's mother, giving Jill to understand that if this had not been the truth she would now have learned the full story of Hugh Lampton's past.

She was about to go, when Mrs. Felton rose to her feet.

"I must find Sister," she said. "I can't take this blanket home as it is. I must have a bit of brown paper for it. And some string to tie it up."

As she spoke she fingered a white blanket that was lying in a heap on the table.

"What is it?" asked Jill.

"The ambulance men brought Chris here in it. Under their own blankets. It must be one of Hugh's. Sister wants me to take it away, now that I'm going home."

"Have you been here all the time since he came in?" Jill asked, with a feeling of pity for this genuine devotion.

"Of course," answered Mrs. Felton, opening wide eyes. "He might have been dying."

"I'll fold it up for you," offered Jill, "while you find Sister and that piece of brown paper."

Jill went home to Hampstead feeling pleased with herself, and a good deal excited.

"Any luck?" asked David. "You look as if you'd had some."

"Yes. Darling, get out your medical directory again, and look through the Rs."

"Why?"

"A blanket of Lampton's was at the hospital. It had initials in one corner. I saw them when Mrs. Felton went off to find Sister."

"You looked for them, you mean. Good girl. What were they?"

"H.L.R. Hugh Lampton R-something. Perhaps."

"We'll see."

But there was no surname beginning with R that carried the first names Hugh or Lampton.

"You'll have to look through the old directories again, won't you?"

David agreed. He found time to do this in his lunch hour at St. Edmund's the next day, after which he got in touch with the Registrar's office. Then he rang up Jill.

"Congratulations!" he said. "For what it is worth there was a Hugh Lampton Redford practising in Sussex ten years ago. He was struck off for infamous conduct in a professional sense."

"What does that mean?"

"Tell you later."

That evening Jill renewed the question.

"It usually means a woman patient," said David. "I didn't want to go into detail on the hospital 'phone. You never know if the telephonists are interested."

"You said quite a lot."

"They wouldn't register the name. It came before the scandal."

"A woman?" said Jill, thoughtfully. "That was what Mrs. Felton said."

Chapter XI

DAVID WINTRINGHAM'S work at St. Edmund's Hospital prevented him for the rest of that week from giving any attention to Hugh Lampton's doubtful past. But on Sunday evening he announced to Jill that they would spend the following week-end in the country.

" Where? " she asked.

" At Tillingham. Small town on the edge of the Ashdown Forest."

" Tillingham. Where have I heard that name before? "

" In this room. A few days ago. Dr. Hugh Lampton Redford, The Pines, Tillingham, Sussex."

" Of course. What are we going to do there? "

" Go down on Friday evening. I'll fix a room at the pub. There is a local newspaper, thank God. On Saturday I hope to get a look at past numbers."

" I see. What do I do? "

" Make friends with the pub staff and find out if they remember the scandal."

Jill made a face at him. It did not seem to her that the week-end would be altogether a pleasant one.

" Darling," she said, presently, " how far is this Tillingham from Limpsfield? "

" Miles, I should think. Why? "

" Because Angela and Charles live between there and the Ashdown Forest. And if they were near enough to take an interest, it might be much more rewarding to talk to them than to the hotel staff, who are probably temporary, coming from London or Ireland."

" True. I'll get the map."

This suggested that their friends did indeed live within easy reach of Tillingham; about eight miles from the little town. It was decided that on Saturday, while David was consulting the local newspaper editor, Jill would drive over to see them, provided they were home that week-end.

In this the Wintringhams were fortunate. Angela, rung up from 'The White Hart' in Tillingham, expressed delighted surprise. Why didn't they both come? Jill would tell her next day. A job, was it? They knew what that meant. They would be thrilled.

But though Jill explained exactly what she wanted to know, she did not tell her friends its possible implications. Angela was not very helpful.

"Ten years ago!" she exclaimed. "How on earth do you expect me to remember one scandal from another as long ago as that? Besides, we can only just have come here. Charles was demobbed in '46, I brought the children down from Scotland a couple of months later, and we decided to live in the country, as the London house had gone for a burton. Yes, we must just have settled in here when your doctor blotted his copy book."

"And you don't remember hearing about it?" said Jill, beginning to be disappointed.

"Not a thing," answered Angela, cheerfully. "But wait till Charles gets back. He'll be in any minute now. Though he works in London every day, he knows every single thing that happens in the district, and for miles round. A real gossip column, Charles. It's the hour in the train, with his business buddies. They pretend to read their newspapers. Actually, they exchange all the latest titbits of local excitement."

Angela was right. Charles thought for a moment and then produced the story.

"Redford. Yes. Been doctoring in the army during the war. Did rather well, I believe, in the Normandy landings. Took over a practice belonging to a chap that was killed in the Navy. Very popular with all the old ladies. That didn't matter. It was when he started to be popular with the young ones that trouble began. Now let me see. Yes, I remember. A chap called—can't remember the name. Was attached

to Town and Country Planning; post-war effort to
rearrange the whole country on a convenient blue print.
Waste of time, naturally. It couldn't work in a country like
this. But the poor chap was doing his best to keep some
sense in it. His wife was thought to be a bit peculiar. Did
you never hear anything about her, Angie? I should have
thought it would be right up your street. Or any way,
Jean's."

"No," said his wife. "No bells ring."

"She was always in the doctor's surgery. That didn't
surprise anyone. But they were surprised the doctor fell for
her."

"Was she so unattractive?"

"I never met her," said Charles. "The general idea was
she had nothing special about her at all, in looks, character
or anything else. But the chief surprise was that the doctor
risked his career for a woman like that. He ought to have
known better. He ought to have known the husband better,
anyway."

"I see."

"My own feeling, only from other people's accounts, mind
you, is that the fellow jumped at the chance of getting rid
of her."

"He divorced her?"

Both Angela and Charles stared at Jill.

"But—but wasn't that *why* you want to know? The
divorce?"

Jill laughed. They were sitting in the garden, looking
across the valley at a range of low hills, with beyond the blue-
grey line of the distant South Downs. The Sussex air was
mild, and fragrant with the scent of wallflowers. On such an
afternoon sordid little family tragedies seemed absurd as well
as deplorable.

"No," she said. "But it clears up a good deal. Dr. Redford was called as co-respondent, and that led to his being
struck off the register. Doctors can be immoral like the rest,
and they will only get a bad name, and probably reduce their
practice. But if they take advantage of their professional

standing to seduce a patient, they are for it, and quite right, too."

"The idea at the time," said Charles, "was that the doctor chap let himself in for this to cover up a worse scandal, that would have ditched his practice completely. At any rate he never married the woman."

"No," said Jill. "He doesn't appear to be married. And he did ditch the practice."

"I think that's thoroughly stingy," complained Angela. "You invite yourself here, having refused several of our invitations to come down; you eat our food, and drink our best sherry, you pick Charles's brains and force him to remember, or more probably invent, a splendid Sunday newspaper story, and then you won't tell us why you know this defrocked doctor, and how well you know him, and what he's been up to, to make you, or I suppose it's David, stir up this lovely mud again."

"Perhaps David will tell you," answered Jill. "We want you to come in to 'The White Hart' for dinner to-night, if you will. Or lunch to-morrow."

And with that she changed the subject, and no effort on their part could bring her back to it.

Meanwhile David had made the acquaintance of the editor of the local paper, who was inclined to be sceptical, but was proud of his ability to produce well-ordered files of his past numbers.

"You're lucky," he said. "Our storage space here is limited, and we recently got rid of a lot of the pre-war stuff. We can't go on indefinitely, like the British Museum. We've got it down to a system, now. Each year we sort out any special numbers, giving outstanding events, and file them on the top of that year. Each year we get rid of one year, ten years back, but keep these top copies. Get the idea?"

"Splendid," said David. "So you won't have destroyed 1947 yet, or will you?"

"No," answered the editor, smiling. "You're just in time."

"Would my case be among the important top copies?"

"No." The editor was mildly shocked. "That sort of thing sells the paper at the time, but it is not exactly an event of historical interest to the town, is it?"

"I suppose not. If it had been a new sewage works——"

"Quite."

"So I may have rather a search?"

"Not if you have your dates. My files are in chronological order."

"Fine."

With this encouragingly well-organized material, David's task was easy. The case, reported in full, appeared in only one issue. It had been undefended. Tufnell v. Tufnell and Redford. There was an inset photograph of Redford, bearing, as expected, a good likeness to the man David knew as Hugh Lampton. There was no picture of Mrs. Tufnell. When David had made a few notes of the case, he went back to the editor.

"No picture of Mrs. Tufnell?" he asked.

The editor shook his head.

"Mr. Tufnell saw me personally, and asked me to spare him the added indignity," he said. "She was no beauty, as you may know. I was quite content to oblige the poor fellow. It was bad enough for his career having to divorce her. Anyway, she would not have made a glamorous picture," he added, his virtuous attitude breaking down as he remembered Mrs. Tufnell.

David laughed.

"Can you describe her to me?" he asked.

"Like thousands of other women," answered the editor. "Medium height and build. Round sort of face, not much animation, except when she got excited. Which she was liable to do over trifles, I understand. Nobody could understand the infatuation. If there was any. On the doctor's side, I mean. *She* was infatuated, all right."

"If he hadn't reciprocated, why didn't he defend himself? Doctors have to defend themselves fairly often against this sort of thing. And quite successfully, as often as not."

"I don't think he was in a position to defend himself. If the mud had been stirred in good and proper, too much would have come up. She wasn't the only one, by any means."

"He lost pretty heavily, all the same."

"Being struck off, you mean? Well, he hasn't done too badly since, by all accounts."

David seized on this.

"By *whose* accounts?"

The editor shook his head.

"Don't go making a mystery of that. Redford was practising here only just over two years, but he was a chap who made friends easily. He was—sort of—impressive, if you know what I mean?"

David knew very well. He nodded.

"So quite a number of his acquaintances in Tillingham, I won't say they were friends, kept up with him. Some of the ladies too, followed him to London as patients. Even after the Health Service started, a good few of them went on going to him, and still do. I don't know how they can afford it."

David said nothing to this. He knew the hold a psychologist can have on his patients. And these women might not depend on Lampton only for psychological comfort. Chris Felton was a drug addict, that was pretty obvious. So why not some of these others?

"What about Tufnell?" he asked, to change the subject.

"Oh, his job here came to an end, and he got himself transferred. He married again, I believe. People say that was all fixed up before the divorce proceedings began, but you know what people are. The law made no complaints."

"And Redford pushed off to London. What happened to Mrs. Tufnell?"

"I don't know. She vanished from this town before the case came on, and took the boy with her."

"The boy?"

"Tufnell's son. He must have been about twelve when his mother was divorced."

David was astonished.

"You mean to say this man Tufnell allowed a boy of twelve to go with his mother in those circumstances? He had every right in law to keep him."

"It did cause a considerable amount of comment. But there again it was thought the second Mrs. Tufnell wanted a clean break. And the boy was known to be devoted to his mother, and she to him."

"Is that so?"

David thanked the editor and left him. It had been a profitable visit, indeed.

Later, at 'The White Hart', David and Jill compared notes. It was gratifying to find that their separate information tallied so exactly.

"All the same," said Jill, "I don't see how this has any connection with the present time. Still less with the murder of Oswald Burke."

"Except that both Charles and the editor hinted at even darker things in Redford's life. Isn't it possible Burke knew of them, too?"

"In which case you were right when you said Burke might have threatened to expose Lampton Redford, unless he laid off Chris Felton."

"Felton," said David, thoughtfully. "Now would you say Mrs. Felton was a very ordinary-looking woman, with a round face, middle height and weight?"

"A bit above middle weight, I should say. Definitely plump."

"In ten years she may have put on a bit."

"Oh!" cried Jill. "And a devoted son and all! Do you think Mrs. Felton is really Mrs. Tufnell?"

"I just wondered. Divorced women often change their name. I remember Lampton told me Chris had lost his father when he was twelve. It fits."

It was an interesting idea, they both thought, but it still did not lead anywhere.

"Unless," said Jill, "Chris had it in for Lampton all these years, on account of his not marrying his mother, and the boy has been waiting his chance."

"For what? It was Burke who was killed, not Lampton."

"No. Of course. If Chris killed Burke it would have to be to defend Lampton, or himself, or both, wouldn't it?"

"Yes, it would."

"Anyway, Mrs. Felton talks quite calmly about Hugh, as she calls him."

They were silent for a time, then Jill asked, "Are you going to see Steve about all this?"

"I rang him up before we came away. He said he knew all he needed to know about Lampton's past. He wouldn't say what he meant by that."

"Sounds like bluff."

"Steve isn't much given to bluff. He probably meant he was not in the least interested in Lampton."

"What are we going to do, now?"

"I can't see anything we can do. Except wait for fresh developments. Chris will go to stay with his mother when they discharge him from hospital. Personally I think some-one tried to do him in. I don't think it was suicide."

"Lampton?"

"Possibly. Though I can't see any point in that, yet. Not Tom. He hadn't been near him since the fire. Except the time Chris went to the pub. Tom thinks Chris arranged the fire. Again, that may have been Lampton."

"Or Mrs. Felton. Especially if she is Mrs. Tufnell."

David shook his head and began to fill a pipe.

"Too complicated," he said. "Stick to essentials. Chief of which is that Bert Lewis's trial is coming on soon. Steve says Lewis still swears he didn't steal the gold cigarette-case from the corpse. Or the wallet. He didn't steal anything except the money in the safe. He confesses to the safe job, now. If he happens to be speaking the truth for once, how did that case come to be where he says it was."

"Where exactly was that?"

"In one of the passages running behind the room where the body was found. It leads up from the lavatories on that side."

"Lampton was in the Gents, wasn't he? Didn't those television people say so? He would have to get to the main door by that passage." *appropriately, a back passage*

Chapter XII

LIONEL PARKINGTON, Q.C., was not at all happy about the Bert Lewis case. He had agreed to undertake the little man's defence because he was genuinely convinced that his client was innocent of murder, indeed quite incapable of it. Besides, he had no real motive.

Lewis was crooked, an incorrigible thief from his youth up. But he was an experienced thief, and often successful. Obviously he had made some plan before he went to the Gallery. He knew where and how he could lay his hands on the sum of money he had decided to take. And he had carried out his plan successfully. Now, that must have been after the Gallery was closed for the day. Tom Drummond had seen Lewis in the hall just before closing time. Later, he must have gone to some hiding-place to wait until everyone was out of the building. Suppose Oswald Burke, with his known inquisitiveness, had gone into the room under reconstruction, to see how the work was progressing? Suppose he found Lewis there? Bert was a practised liar. Nothing would have been easier for him than to invent a plausible excuse for his presence, and one that Burke would probably accept without question. Overtime, something of that sort. He had been wearing dungarees in Tom's sketch. Quite in character. It was fantastic to suppose either that Burke would immediately conclude the man was a criminal, or that he would accuse him of it to his face, or that Lewis would retaliate with violence. On the other hand Lewis had got possession of the dead man's gold cigarette-case, in addition to bringing off his planned burglary.

The cigarette-case was, of course, the crux of the matter. Parkington was prepared to put forward a theory that Burke, with his propensity to inquire into and criticize other people's

work and plans, might very well have climbed on to the
scaffolding to inspect the upper part of the new wall-covering
at close range. He might have fallen, and broken his neck.
And afterwards Lewis might have found the corpse and
robbed it. But when Parkington suggested this story to the
little man, he rejected it with almost hysterical vehemence.
Lewis insisted that his own explanation was the true
one.

So when David Wintringham asked for an interview with
counsel on the subject of Bert Lewis, Parkington was very
ready to see him.

"I'm not a new witness for you," David told him. "At
least, I hope not. But I don't think the prosecution has a
case."

"I don't think I've much of one, either," said Parkington,
gloomily. "Is that all you want to tell me?"

"Of course not. I've been in touch with Superintendent
Mitchell all along, and he has told me what Lewis said about
the cigarette-case when they arrested him. He dismisses that
explanation as one of Lewis's more futile lies. But I'm not
so sure. What exactly did Lewis tell you?"

"What did Mitchell tell you?" asked Parkington,
cautiously. "I'd rather start that way round, if you don't
mind."

"Lewis said he found the case in a corridor of the Gallery."

"That all he said?"

"Apparently. But he sticks to it."

"He sticks to it, all right. He even makes it sound a bit
sillier still. He says he picked it up and tried to give it to
someone belonging to the Gallery, but they wouldn't take
it!"

"Does he describe this person?"

"It was a woman. He won't or can't give any detail of her
appearance, or their conversation. His imagination has
not been as lively as usual, with a murder charge on his
head."

"It may not be imagination. I think his story may be
true."

Mr. Parkington showed his surprise and unbelief in no uncertain fashion, but when David had given him a brief outline of his own investigations up to date, he began to take the idea more seriously.

"I suppose Superintendent Mitchell knows what you are doing?" he asked.

"Up to a point. But he thinks I am wasting my time. He has no objection to that."

"I see. Really, you are trying to find someone with an adequate murder motive, aren't you?"

"That's it. I don't think Lewis had one."

"There we are working together. My defence rests on that." He smiled ruefully. "It has damned little else to rest on."

David looked thoughtful.

"If only Lewis wasn't such a dumb cluck," he said, at length. "And such a hopeless character, in every way. Old lag, mean as they come, a moral and physical coward, a liar who doesn't know by now when he's lying and when he isn't. Not much hope of getting anything useful out of him. But I want detail. Exact detail of what really happened about that cigarette-case. If he did meet a woman in that corridor, she wasn't one of the staff at the Gallery. We do know that. She must have been a visitor."

"Lewis did talk to his wife," Parkington said. "She told me so. She told the police different. Said she knew nothing whatever about Bert's affairs, before or after. But he did talk to her that night he went home before he tried to skip abroad. She confirms his story. But of course she may have decided to support him after she knew he was on a capital charge."

"I might go and see her myself," David suggested.

Lionel Parkington agreed to that.

Mrs. Lewis was quite ready to talk to David. She was prepared to clutch at any helping hand in the desperate situation in which she found herself. For years she had built up an existence separate from her criminal husband in all but the legal tie. He spent so little time at home that the neighbours scarcely knew him. She had forced them to recognize her own respectability. Her friends supported her readily enough, with admiration and affection. She had also won a similar respect for her children, taking pride in the fact that they belonged to her world and not Bert's. And now the whole edifice had fallen. The newspapers had seen to that. Their sensational, sentimental, exaggerated accounts of her private life, its struggles, fears, and triumphs, had done her more harm in the eyes of those around her than any of Bert's convictions and prison sentences in the last fifteen years.

"Making a good thing out of it, ain't she? "

"Cashin' in on 'er troubles."

"Disgraceful, the things she's told them."

It was not true, but Mrs. Lewis was not in a position to take an action for libel against those who put false words and sentiments into her mouth for the entertainment of the masses. She had to endure it all. And she was breaking under the strain.

David Wintringham found a haggard-faced, subdued woman, whom Superintendent Mitchell would barely have recognized. She sat opposite him in her well-kept sitting-room, twisting her overall in her hands and from time to time fumbling in its pocket for her handkerchief, to wipe away the tears that kept welling up in her eyes.

"I don't think your husband is guilty of murder," David told her, in a very firm voice. "But I do think he found the body, and robbed it."

"Not that gold case," said Mrs. Lewis at once. "I swear to God Almighty, not the case! "

"How can you prove that? You have said in a signed statement that you didn't know anything about the case."

"I told them I didn't know 'e'd put it in the girl's bed," protested Mrs. Lewis. "That's all they asked. 'Didn't I know it was there? ' Well, I didn't, see. I thought 'e'd took it with 'im. I can swear that, honest."

"But you told Mr. Parkington a story about how Bert got it."

"That's right. Bert said 'e'd 'ad a bit of luck, only 'e didn't know if 'e could cash in on it, on account of the initials."

"Go on."

"'E said 'e'd picked up a valuable on the floor at 'is job. Mind you, I never knew then 'e 'ad a job, nor 'e'd lost it, nor where it was, or wot it was. 'E doesn't tell me much. 'E said this valuable was lying there, and 'e picked it up, and give it back to the lady that dropped it."

"Oh, she dropped it, did she?"

"That's 'ow 'e put it. But she wouldn't take it. Told 'im it warn't 'ern, and she didn't want to 'ave nothing to do with it. Bert thought she was balmy."

"Is that all?"

Mrs. Lewis, under the stimulus of kindness and confession, regained something of her old manner.

"Wot more do you want? 'E didn't take it. 'E was give it."

"More fool him to keep it, in those circumstances. But you know he denied the story to the police, at first. Then gave them a rather different version. He said he took the case to a woman belonging to the Gallery staff."

"I don't know nothing of that." She looked suspiciously at David. "You seem to know a 'ell of a lot. Are you on Bert's side, mister, or the copper's?"

"I'm on your side, Mrs. Lewis."

Her tears flowed freely again at that, and David felt he could get nothing more out of her. He wondered what her real relationship with her evil little husband had been, and why she had never made a clean break away from him. She had struggled so hard. Perhaps she was one of those women who must have conflict in their lives. Or perhaps she found satisfaction in a sort of double life, and had even shared secretly in some of Bert's shady operations. Probably she had no very clear ideas at all on morals or conduct; content to drift until sharp demands of one kind or another were

made on her, and then, with her immense vitality
and resilience, rose to meet them. This time, however,
the demands were crushing. That was abundantly
clear.

David got up to go.

"I shall see Bert if I can," he said. "I do believe that his
story is true in the main. I am looking for the real murderer,
and I think if Bert can tell me anything that will help me
to identify this woman, the one he declares gave him the
cigarette-case, we may be on our way to finding the real
criminal. So keep your chin up. Mr. Parkington is doing
his best, and that is quite a lot, you know."

She got up from her chair with a weary dignity that
touched him deeply. He left her, standing framed in the
doorway, a massive Niobe, treading the ruins of her
hopes.

Bert Lewis himself was more difficult, but in the end, more
rewarding. Parkington managed to arrange an interview
for David with the prisoner, and the two men went to see
him together.

Lewis was sullen and obstinate, as very frightened men
usually are. He ignored David at first, merely complain-
ing that Parkington was wasting his time if he expected him
to say he'd robbed a corpse. He'd never seen the bloody
corpse. If he had he'd have left it flat. He wasn't such a
dope as to risk being seen with it. Did they take him for
a fool? It was a frame-up. Deliberate. They wanted
him sent down for good. For something he'd never
done.

His visitors waited patiently until the long slow tirade
came to an end. Then David said, "When you picked up
that gold cigarette-case, was there anyone else in the
corridor?"

Lewis gulped and was silent.

"Did you simply come across it, or did you see her drop
it?"

"I didn't see nothing."

" Except the case. We know you saw that because you had it. Your evidence is that you found it."

" That's right. It was laying there, and I picked it up, and she——"

" Well? "

" She was just turning the corner ahead of me."

" You waited till she turned it before you picked up the case."

Lewis's little red-rimmed eyes flashed angrily.

" I never said that."

" I'm saying it. What happened then? "

" She come back. So I offered it to 'er, see."

" You had it in your hand, so she knew you had picked it up? "

There was no answer to this.

" How do you know it was the same person who came back round the corner? "

" By the clothes and that."

" Can you describe her? "

" Why should I? "

Mr. Parkington intervened here to explain to the unwilling Lewis exactly how important it was for him to co-operate with them. The barrister took over the questioning and in the end got some sort of description of the unknown woman. Dark loose coat, small dark hat, untidy grey hair. He could not say what her face was like.

" Was it like this? " asked David. " Or this? "

He laid before Lewis an open sketch book and a photograph. The answer was disappointing.

" Are they supposed to be the same? "

" No they are not. Do they look the same? "

" I dunno."

Lewis yawned slowly, making no effort to cover his widening mouth. He was bored. But David insisted.

" That's more like," he said, pointing at the drawing. " But the one in the photo 'asn't got no 'at on, so I dunno."

" The clothes in the drawing are like your description, aren't they? "

" Could be."

It was little enough to go upon, but worth pursuing, David thought. There was one more thing he must know.

" What time was it when you found the cigarette-case? " he asked.

" Just on closing time. They were turning the public out."

" And this woman wouldn't take the case? But she didn't tell you to take it to the porter? "

" That's right."

" Did she behave as if it belonged to her? "

" She said I could keep it. I took it she was entitled to make me a present of it."

" Oh, surely! " Parkington controlled his temper with an effort. If Lewis was going to invent this sort of obvious tripe, it would be worse than useless to put him in the witness box. " People don't give away gold cases as if they were boiled sweets! "

" It's the truth! Wot's the use of telling the truth if you don't believe it! "

Bert's face was shiny with fear and indignation. David cut in again.

" So this was just on closing time. Did you leave the Gallery then? "

" Near enough."

" When you picked up this case, was it before or after you stole the money? "

" O.K. Before. 'Ow could I do the job till the place was quiet? "

" When you picked up this case, was it before or after you found the body? "

Bert Lewis's face whitened with anger. He gripped the sides of his chair.

" Well, was it? " David insisted.

But Lewis refused to look at him or to answer the question. With his eyes fixed on his counsel he repeated hoarsely, again and again, " Take 'im out of 'ere, mister! 'E's nothing but a bloody copper like the rest. Take 'im away! Take 'im away! "

"Answer the question," said Parkington, calmly, quite unmoved by his client's outburst.

"I never found no body," Lewis moaned, in a frenzy of exasperation. "'Ow many times 'ave I got to say it? D'you think I'd 'ave gone on with the job if I'd known 'e was there? Wot d'you take me for? Answer me that!"

Chapter XIII

WITH Christopher Felton out of danger, though still under treatment at the hospital for his addiction, Tom Drummond settled down to a spell of concentrated work. All the up-heavals and hazards he had undergone since the fateful afternoon at the Westminster Gallery, far from upsetting his mental and nervous balance, had stimulated him to an intensity of effort that surprised everyone, including himself. With the egotism of the true artist, he had absorbed his experiences, turning them to his own purpose and profit. As David Wintringham had said, he was finding himself, and beginning to realize his powers in terms that he still only dimly understood, but in which he gained an ever increasing self-confidence.

Pauline Manners, watching his progress with the unselfish dedicated love that she would always give him, rejoiced in his new forceful activity, though it meant her own partial exclusion. But here she was helped by her growing friend-ship with the Wintringhams. Jill very much admired her devotion to Tom, and her modesty over her own talent, which, though small, was fresh and charming. During the week, she was not much seen at the house in Hampstead. But at the week-ends, when she had no work to do, she went there during the day, and would sit patiently for hours in the studio while Tom worked. He liked to have her there, even when he forgot her presence.

The Wintringhams lent her books to read, and, as the weather grew warmer, Jill persuaded her to sit in the garden rather than upstairs. This tranquil, uneventful life suited Pauline, who had shared hitherto the restlessness of her generation. Her looks improved: her sallow paleness was replaced by a faint glow that added to the natural beauty of her dark hair and eyes. The Wintringhams did not conceal their admiration, and Pauline's self-confidence grew in consequence.

On the Saturday following David's visit to Bert Lewis in prison, Jill and Pauline were stretched in deck chairs, enjoying a warm sun, when Tom came out of the house to join them. He was looking pale and upset. He flung himself on the ground beside Pauline, and stayed there, silent, not looking at the two women, who exchanged glances of surprise and alarm. They expected some outburst, but none came. Instead, after a time he muttered, "I'm fed up with that flipping butcher."

He meant Symington-Cole, Jill concluded, and smiled at the description.

"Has James been for another sitting?" she asked. "I thought you'd finished with them."

"No. He hasn't been. I want to finish the thing. I ought to have finished it by now. I've had all the time in the world, since I came here." He suddenly smiled up at Jill, a boyish open smile of pure gratitude. "But it's dead. Dead as mutton. He doesn't interest me. He's cold, and callous, and a go-getter. I'm sorry, Jill, if he's a friend of yours."

"It's all right," she told him. "He is all those things, but he is a brilliant surgeon besides, and hundreds of people owe their sight to him, which makes up for it, I think. If a man's work is valuable and creative, I don't think his personal qualities matter very much. Except to his family," she added, with honesty.

"I hope you're right," said Tom. "But it doesn't make it any easier to paint his ugly mug, when I want to get on with the real thing."

"Such as?" asked Pauline.

"You know. You've had a peek at it. I'm not such a bum I can't tell when my things have been tampered with."

Pauline's face reddened, but Jill came to her help.

"I'm afraid we've all had a look at your work," she said. "And I hope you'll take it as a measure of our interest and admiration, and not merely curiosity."

Tom had no answer to this. Besides, he found he did not really care. What he had done was inevitable: the pictures were an expression of his deeply felt shock and disgust at the manner of the critic's death.

"I can't get the foul business out of my mind," he said. "I wish they'd settle it once and for all."

He got to his feet and, stretching out a hand to Pauline, pulled her up from her chair.

"Come on," he said, roughly. "Time to go and see Chris."

It was only too plain that his thoughts of the murder led him on to his former friend. Did he now believe, in spite of its inherent improbability, that Chris Felton was the criminal? Jill wondered. Was it that, and not Symington-Cole's unsympathetic personality, that had upset him? She watched the pair go off hand in hand. Pauline might get to the root of the trouble, and if so, would tell her later on.

David came home early that afternoon and joined his wife in the garden. She told him about Tom's change of mood.

"He's worrying about Chris Felton, I'm sure. Did Chris do it?"

"How do I know? I'm worrying about Bert Lewis. Obstinate fool."

"Why don't you talk to Tom about Lewis? Anything to get him back to James's picture. It's so important for him. He can't earn his living by painting symbols of horror and fear."

"Several painters have. But never mind that. I know what you mean. It probably isn't Tom's real line. He seems to me too robust a character to have a permanent preoccupation with death. I'll do what you say."

So, later that evening, when Tom and Pauline got back to Hampstead after seeing Chris at the hospital, they were intercepted by David, who asked them in for a drink. Jill noticed that Tom looked much more cheerful.

"How was Chris?" she asked, deliberately direct.

"Better." Tom looked at Pauline, who nodded. "They're getting him off his addiction," he said, flatly.

"Do you know what it was?" David asked. He had suspected dope, earlier. It was interesting to find Tom quite open about it.

"I'm not sure. Nor where he gets it. I've always suspected Lampton. He gave him a lot of that stuff they use to make their patients talk freely. I think Chris got to depend on it, and Lampton fed it to him to keep him on the books."

"Could be. Incidentally," said David, seizing this very lucky opening, "I was going to ask you one or two things about Lampton. If you remember, you said you had destroyed a drawing of him. Then you said Chris destroyed it. Which was it?"

This was a deliberate mistake on David's part. He waited for an explosion, but Tom only said, quietly, "Not Lampton. You mean Burke, don't you?"

"Of course, yes. When you first came here you said you had removed it. That was the first one, the mild ordinary one. Why did you tear it out?"

"I didn't."

"As you said at the Yard. That is the true story, is it?"

"Yes."

"Felton destroyed it because he had this thing against Burke?"

"Presumably."

"Would it surprise you to know that Felton denies taking out that drawing?"

"It would not. Look, David, it's been eating me ever since it happened. Whether Chris could have killed him. He's so hysterical, and so tied up with that trick cyclist and this addiction of his. I don't honestly know what he mightn't have done. At least, that's the way I was feeling until I saw him to-day. He's a hell of a lot better. Quieter. More rational. He wanted to talk about Burke. The first time he hasn't bawled me out if I started to mention him. And he said something I was going to tell you, anyhow."

"What's that?"

"He said it was Lampton put him up to tearing out the

drawing of Burke, but he refused, because it was my work. So obviously Lampton must have done it, really."

"That sounds very possible."

"He wanted Chris to destroy another one, too. The one of him and Chris together."

"Did he, indeed?"

David got out the drawings, and turned the pages of the book until he reached the one of Felton and Lampton. Tom was looking at it, too, and it was Tom who remarked, with mild surprise, "I seem to have filled up with a good many bits and pieces, don't I?"

This was true. At the top of the page were Chris and Hugh Lampton, facing each other, Chris partly turned towards the artist, Lampton partly turned away. Below, there was a medley of legs and feet, at rest and moving, together with several parts of faces.

"There!" exclaimed David. "Why didn't I see it before? It's that woman again!"

"What woman?"

"Look!"

Tom turned the pages back and forward, considering, remembering, listening to David's account of the Bert Lewis story, and the Ellis story, and finally, the Lampton story.

"Who is she? Is it this woman he ditched himself over? This Mrs. Tufnell?"

"Could be, don't you think?"

"Why have I made her look like Burke?"

"Tom," said David, gently. "Why do all your latest pictures look like Burke?"

A strange light came into Tom's eyes, but his voice was as quiet as David's own.

"I just see things that way at present." He paused, looking round at Pauline, to see what she thought of this. Her face was troubled, and she said, "But, Tom, you did that face before you knew what had happened! I mean, before anything *had* happened."

"Correct," said Tom. He turned back to David. "What do you make of that?" he asked, defiantly.

"Nothing. The main snag to getting anywhere is that Lewis, the mule, won't or can't say if she is the woman he swears gave him the cigarette-case. Or, rather, told him to keep it. I took him down these drawings, and a photo of Mrs. Felton I borrowed from Chris. Bert agreed the clothes were like, but wouldn't swear to the face."

"Chris never told me he'd lent you a photo of his mum," interrupted Tom.

"He may not have noticed yet that he has lent it to me. I don't think he saw it go. Anyway, I took Lewis the photo and the drawings, and he said it might have been either. I ask you!"

Looking at the photograph, and then again at the sketches, Tom agreed that Lewis was definitely not trying. The two women were alike in build and of a similar type, but their features were quite different, their hair also, and nothing could have been less alike than their style of dress.

"Not that it pins anything down, does it?" asked Pauline, who had listened hard to the whole conversation.

"No," David answered. "It makes the whole affair creak worse than ever."

On the following Monday, however, Superintendent Mitchell's inquiries, set off by David's account to him of his activities and by his own views on the fire, and Felton's possible suicide attempt, began to pay off handsomely, though not at all as that harassed officer could wish. It was reported to him that Mrs. Tufnell's maiden name was Burke. She was the only sister of Oswald Burke. Mitchell passed this information on to David Wintringham.

"Burke," said David. "Why didn't I know he had a sister?"

"You could have asked, as I did. But you had to have these highbrow ideas on art."

"*Touché!* Tom, the photographer, after all!"

"Exactly."

"Burke's sister, seduced by Redford, alias Lampton,

divorced by Tufnell, subsequently discarded by the lover. What about it, Steve? "

"I suppose you mean she might be bitter against Lampton. Or Tufnell. I don't see any other inference."

"What did Oswald feel about Lampton? Did he interfere at all in the case? It would be in character for him to do so. Was it, perhaps, his fault that Lampton wouldn't marry his sister after the divorce? "

"Are you suggesting Mrs. Tufnell murdered her brother? "

"If he wrecked her affair I am suggesting she had a much better motive than Bert Lewis."

David got no answer to this.

"Steve! Are you still there, Steve? You'll have to find out what Mrs. Tufnell was doing at the Westminster, won't you? She was certainly there that Wednesday. Did she go to see her brother, or Lampton? Or did she just happen to be there when they drifted in? Only that would be an almighty coincidence, wouldn't it? "

"I'm not convinced she was there," said Mitchell. "She's been in some sort of private institution for years."

"Ah. I heard she had a breakdown. It was permanent, was it? "

"Get off the line, damn you," said the Superintendent. "I have work to do."

Unwillingly, but from a sense of duty that gave him no rest, Mitchell set in motion further inquiries into the life and circumstances and present whereabouts of Mrs. Barbara Tufnell. These he left to others. He went in person to Lampton's consulting rooms.

The latter impressed him very favourably, as he did most people. He frowned a little when Mitchell explained who he was, and why he had come, but he was perfectly willing to answer questions. He agreed to all that Mitchell stated about his former relations with Mrs. Tufnell. He offered no additional information on the subject.

"Did you meet her at the Gallery by accident, or by arrangement? " Mitchell asked.

"Quite by accident. I had not seen her for many years. I was surprised and rather shocked to find she wanted to speak to me."

"Do you think she went there on purpose to see you? If so, how did she know you would be there?"

"She could not have known in advance," said Lampton, firmly. "I only made up my mind to go when a patient cancelled an appointment. Young Felton asked me to join him there, so I did that."

"I understand. Perhaps she went to see her brother."

"That is much more probable. He always took an interest in her, I know. Though she was not on good terms with him."

"Why not?"

"He was very much opposed to the divorce at the time. Did his best to get a reconciliation."

"What was your reaction to that?"

Lampton raised his eyebrows.

"It was hardly my place to have a reaction, was it?"

"In the circumstances," said Mitchell, dryly, "perhaps not. In view of the fact that you had no intention of marrying her."

Lampton gave him a quick, angry look, but said nothing.

"One thing more," said Mitchell, quietly. "You were noticed waiting on the Embankment when the Gallery was just about closing——"

"Who the devil?"

"Never mind who. You were seen and have since been identified. Can you tell me who you were waiting for? Mrs. Tufnell?"

"I spoke to her when she came out. Yes."

"You have not answered my question. I'll put it another way. Was Christopher Felton still in the Gallery at that time?"

"I don't know."

"Then you were not waiting for him?"

"I did not say so."

"We shall not get anywhere by stalling, Mr. Lampton. You were waiting for someone to come out. Felton? "

"Yes."

"Did he come? "

"Mrs. Tufnell came. She insisted upon talking to me."

"Where? At the foot of the steps? "

"No. We moved away along the Embankment."

"And Felton? "

"He joined me—later."

"How much later? "

"I don't remember."

"And spoke to you and Mrs. Tufnell? "

"No. She had gone by then."

"How long was this conversation? Half an hour? "

"I tell you, I don't remember."

"If it was more then ten minutes the Gallery must have been closed. How do you know that Felton came out of it *after* Mrs. Tufnell? Or after you, for that matter? Why not before? He could have gone away up the road and come back, couldn't he? "

Lampton swallowed uneasily. His throat seemed to have gone very dry.

"Yes. Yes, I suppose he could."

"Mr. Lampton, you know as well as I do that Christopher Felton left the Gallery before you did. And that he did not come back at all. You stayed to speak to Mrs. Tufnell, and to her alone."

Lampton simply stared at him. There was no anger, no protest, no fear in that stony face. Is he wondering what I have got out of young Felton, Mitchell thought, or is he wondering why the boy left the Westminster without telling him where he was going? Has he been wondering this all along? No, obviously not. Felton went away to avoid Mrs. Tufnell. He had said so. Lampton knew it, too. But would never acknowledge it. Mitchell knew that the psychiatrist would answer no more questions that day.

K

Chapter XIV

WHEN Oswald Burke's widow was told that Dr. Wintringham wanted to see her again, she was inclined to refuse. Superintendent Mitchell had already called, with most distressing news, and a fresh set of questions that had disquieted her very much indeed. Now the doctor seemed to be following up this new information, though he had no official standing whatever with the police, as the Superintendent had taken pains to impress upon her.

But she remembered that it was Dr. Wintringham, after all, who was wrecking the straightforward case against her husband's murderer, and who had introduced all these fresh complications. For her own protection, perhaps, it would be wise to speak to him. But she kept him waiting a quarter of an hour before she did so.

"This is very good of you," David said, when they had shaken hands. "I had no right to expect it, only that I felt you would really prefer to know more detail, even if it distresses you."

"You want to find out the truth," said Mrs. Burke. "Don't pretend you have any concern for my feelings."

"Yes. I want to find the truth. And I do not want an innocent man punished for something he did not do."

"Naturally," said Mrs. Burke, smoothly. "I share that wish."

David regretted her open hostility, but he could do nothing about it. So he went on, carefully and formally, to take her over the past history of her sister-in-law's affair with Dr. Redford and the subsequent divorce.

"My husband tried his best to prevent that," she said. "But it was hopeless. Geoffrey Tufnell had had enough.

146

More than enough. I don't know why Oswald could not see that."

"How do you mean?"

"Barbara was practically a nymphomaniac. She gave a lot of trouble as a girl. I did not know her then. I only met her when I married Oswald, and she was already married, then. She was more reasonable for a time, until her child was about six. Then she started her old infatuations. Various men. Mostly they were only too anxious to keep away from her. Oswald said it was partly the worry over the child's health, and partly the fact that Geoffrey was too—too cold for her."

Mrs. Burke's handsome face was icy with disgust as she said this. David felt sorry for the late art critic.

"I never could understand why he married her," went on Mrs. Burke. "She did not seem to be at all attractive. But I suppose some men like to have a woman infatuated with them, though most just find it a bore, don't they?"

"I expect so," said David, who had never given this particular subject much thought.

"Personally I always felt rather sorry for poor Dr. Redford. I always wondered if the affair wasn't just a delusion on her part. She boasted of it quite openly. That was the worst of the scandal."

"So I can imagine. But Redford did not defend himself, did he?"

"No. And from all I heard at the time, he did not suffer. Financially, at any rate. He has been more successful as a lay psychiatrist than he was as a general practitioner."

"The margin of error is so much wider," murmured David.

Mrs. Burke laughed. It was not a very pleasant laugh, and David regretted his mild joke.

"Did your husband keep in touch with his sister after the divorce?" he asked.

"Oh, yes. Very much so. You see, she had a breakdown. She was in a mental hospital. Oswald was in charge of her affairs."

This tallied with what Steve had said, David reflected. It might explain much.

"For how long?" he asked.

"I don't remember exactly. I never saw her, myself, afterwards. I—we—never knew each other well."

David looked at her sadly. He could imagine very well the situation that had developed. Oswald Burke, filled with that warm-hearted solicitude for which he was well known, and with a family affection not to be crushed by his wife's opposition, struggling to help his maimed sister, and getting no sympathy at home for his long sustained effort.

"Oswald did not speak much about her. I knew, of course, that he kept in touch."

In touch with his unstable sister, and progressively out of touch with his frigid, impeccable wife, David decided. There was very little more he could hope to learn from her.

"As far as you know, then, Mrs. Tufnell spent some years in hospital?"

"I think it must have been about three. But I really don't remember."

"What happened to the boy?"

Mrs. Burke looked startled for a moment, then recovered her former composure.

"I don't think I ever heard," she said, slowly.

"We know that his father did not take him."

"Oh, no. There was some argument about that. He was left with his mother because he had been ill so much. They had an excellent nurse who understood him very well."

"Do you remember her name?"

Mrs. Burke thought, or made a show of doing so, and then shook her head.

"I'm sorry," she said. "I don't remember."

David said he must go. And now, it seemed, Mrs. Burke did not want the interview to end.

"Superintendent Mitchell would not tell me why these inquiries about Barbara are being made. I find it very disturbing. You started them, didn't you? I think you ought to tell me why."

"I'll do that," David answered. "You know that the case against the old lag, the burglar Bert Lewis, rests on finding your husband's gold cigarette-case in his possession?"

"Yes, I know that."

"Mitchell thinks, or thought, that Lewis robbed the man he had killed. Lewis swears he found the case in a passage at the Gallery. He says he offered it to a woman we now identify as Mrs. Tufnell, and she refused to take it. I happen to believe Lewis's story. I think it is not one he would be likely to invent. And that being so, I want to know two things. Did Mrs. Tufnell have the case and drop it, and if so how had she come by it? And why did she refuse to take it back? If Mrs. Tufnell did not drop it in that corridor, how did it get there? Remembering that Mr. Burke's body was found in a room nearby."

"You seem to have more than two questions there," said Mrs. Burke, rather unsteadily. "Do you think you will find the answers?"

"I shall go on trying. And so will Mitchell. He has better ways of finding out than I have. He'll probably get what he needs from Mrs. Tufnell, herself."

"I wonder," said Mrs. Burke, "if he knows where she is. When I rang up her home last night, after the Superintendent left here——"

"Her home?" said David, quickly.

"A small private guest house for unstable cases. Not certified ones. She was never certified. She was at the mental hospital on a voluntary basis."

"I see. Go on."

"The guest house told me she had gone away to London, but had not left any precise address, nor said when they could expect her back."

Mr. Symington-Cole was getting impatient. He had no idea how long it took an artist to paint a portrait, but judging by the speed with which young Drummond had got the thing going, he thought it should have been finished by now. The sittings were over; had been over a fortnight ago. At that time, when he insisted upon seeing the progress of the work, it looked to him nearly finished. Not finished in the sense he understood real finish. Not like the old masters. But a great deal easier to look at than some of the stuff they hung in the galleries, and even at the Academy, these days. And it was a fair likeness, he considered, though not flattering. This bruised his vanity, but he had to acknowledge that the general impression was one of power and great intellectual ability; and the hands, those all-important surgeon's hands, were beautifully done. In fact, the thing looked finished, and he could not understand why it had not been delivered.

So he wrote a stiff letter to Tom, demanding to have a fixed date by which he could expect the picture to arrive at the Medical School. The Presentation Committee, he said, was getting impatient. They had been good enough to suggest making a little ceremony over hanging the painting in the Library, and they did not want this put off until everyone was away on summer holidays.

Tom showed the letter to Pauline when she arrived at the studio that evening.

"Then why don't they say so, direct?" Tom exploded. "I don't believe a word of it. Cole made that up to drive me."

"But it *is* nearly finished, isn't it?" Pauline asked.

She went to the easel on which the portrait stood and threw back the cloth that covered it.

"Leave it alone!" shouted Tom, suddenly furious. "I hate the sight of the bloody thing!"

Pauline, used to his outbursts, paid no attention, but stood, admiring his work. It was first-class, she thought. At least, nearly first-class. She shared the vague disappointment the Wintringhams had felt the last time they saw it.

"It's good," she said. "Why don't you do what he says? Get it done. Send it away. If you hate it so much, write it off as it is now. They'd never know. It looks finished enough to me."

Tom sprang up and moved quickly to her. She had her hand on the easel, about to pull down the cloth again. He seized her by both arms to whirl her away. He was beside himself with rage.

As she stumbled under the unexpected onslaught, she clutched at the easel to steady herself. Instead of supporting her, it toppled over. Tom, who saw it slip, let go the girl and grabbed at his work instead. He lost his balance, and fell, clutching the canvas, holding it in the air to save it, like a cricketer fielding a difficult catch.

Pauline's yell of laughter as he went down on his back, legs sprawling, arms about his painting, changed to a cry of terror. For the back of the canvas came away in Tom's grasp, and it fell to one side. There were two canvases, she saw, tacked on to the same frame, the second one with its painted side against the back of the eye surgeon's portrait. She snatched it up and stood it on an empty easel under the window.

"Oh, my God!" she whispered, and felt herself grow cold with fear.

It was a picture of Oswald Burke, in the very act of death. His body was falling; his head had already fallen, lying over on his left shoulder, lacking the support of the neck that was broken. All about him jagged shapes and twisted planes mixed and mingled and whirled, as the man's fading world must have whirled and shivered to pieces around him when the blow fell. These menacing shapes crowded upon him, crossing and recrossing the grotesque limp form that fell, constricting it into a narrow path that ran away up behind the contorted neck to a pinpoint of light. The whole was painted in sombre grey and black and purple. Only the point of light and the man's face stood out, startling white and green. And the eyes, wholly natural, staring, alive with horror and a fierce anger.

"My God!" whimpered Pauline, and turned to look at Tom.

He had got to his feet, and when she turned he put back the painting of Symington-Cole very quietly and carefully on its easel, and went over to her. He stood behind her, and put his arms round her, and rested his cheek on her hair.

"Good, don't you think?" he said, in a self-satisfied voice.

She was profoundly shocked. She broke away from him, crying out that it was revolting, loathsome, blasphemous——

"Now why that?" asked Tom, mildly. He was still looking at his work; all of his anger had evaporated. This was the final expression of what he had started to paint from the day of the murder. It was exactly what he meant it to be.

"Blasphemous? Because it's—it's—a sort of total destruction—a sort of wiping out——"

"No future at all?" Tom laughed. "Do you believe in a future life?"

"I don't know. Who does? But that——"

She stopped, forcing herself into control. However much she hated this picture, however much it outraged her feelings and her thoughts, it was Tom's work, and it was remarkable. There was something more that had to be said.

She moved further away from him, towards the door, before she spoke.

"You never did that out of your head," she said. "You saw him, dead. You must have."

Tom drew a long breath.

"You saw him," Pauline repeated, fear driving her voice up to a high note. "You saw him die, or you saw him dead! You only draw what you see. I know that. I've always known it. Dr. Wintringham thinks these awful things you've been painting are development. Development my foot! They're memory. Plain memory. And you couldn't keep it in!"

"Shut up!" said Tom, quickly. He had heard a step on the stairs, and came striding across to her. He took her by the arm and shook her. "Shut up, you hysterical little cat, or I'll——"

She tried to scream, but his hand was over her mouth. The door opened and David Wintringham stood on the threshold.

"Am I interrupting anything?" he asked, pleasantly.

Chapter XV

PAULINE burst into tears and ran blindly from the room and out of the house. In the road she halted, struggling to control herself, but the shock of her discovery was too great: the double discovery was too much for her. Tom was mixed up in the murder after all; whether he had dealt the fatal blow himself or not, he had concealed vital evidence. And he had deceived her, or if not that, he had kept from her something so vital that their mutual trust was now shattered, perhaps for ever. She leaned against the wall, feeling sick and faint, beyond caring who might see her distress.

Quite soon she was aware that someone had noticed her. A woman was standing on the edge of the pavement quite near her. She looked as if she had just crossed the road.

Pauline, making a great effort, straightened up, and then bent over, pretending that she had stopped to empty a stone from her shoe. This done, she straightened again. The woman was still there, watching her.

"I saw you come out of that house," she said.

Pauline waited. She did not want to speak to the woman, but she did not want to turn from her rudely, either. She probably meant to be kind.

"That is Dr. Wintringham's house, isn't it?" the woman went on.

Startled by this wholly unexpected remark, Pauline looked at her questioner more closely. She saw a plain, middle-aged face under a bottle-green felt hat. A loose dark-grey coat hung about a dumpy figure. Pauline, her thoughts running still on Tom's danger and his duplicity, failed to recognize her.

"Yes," she answered, with surprise in her voice. "Do you know him?"

Who would be a doctor, she thought? This must surely

be some devoted patient, perhaps come to bother him at his home. She had learned enough of his routine from Jill to know that his work lay entirely at St. Edmund's Hospital, in the department of clinical research. He had no private practice, as some of the other consultants had. So she added, to protect him, " But he isn't at home. He is at the hospital."

The woman gave a little soft laugh. Pauline felt very uncomfortable. She had been silly to say that. Doubtless the woman had been hanging about for some time, and had seen David go in. She might even have watched him put away his car in the mews at the end of the road. It was not in front of the house, so he must have put it away, not expecting to go back to the hospital that day. At this moment, he was talking to Tom. Tom!

She felt her eyelids pricking with fresh tears, and turned away.

" You seem to be upset," said the woman, in a gentle voice. " Why don't you come home with me for a cup of tea? "

" With *you*? " exclaimed Pauline, stopping dead in her astonishment.

" Why not? "

" I—I don't know you."

" No," said the woman, and sighed. " Well, never mind."

She turned and walked towards the Heath. Pauline watched her. Ought she to go in and tell Jill about this queer old party? She felt inclined to do so. Jill was wonderful with David's more awkward visitors, and the woman might only be waiting until she was out of the way to come back. But Pauline remembered that Tom was still in the house. She could not risk meeting him again. Not yet. Not until she knew——

Very slowly, head bent, the girl went away towards Rosslyn Hill. When she was gone, Mrs. Tufnell, who had kept her in sight from the other end of the road, came back, to take up again her patient watch.

" So that's it, is it? " said David, standing before the picture on the easel. Tom said nothing.

"Where did you see him? Which corridor, or subterranean passage?"

"Why do you say that? He was found in a large exhibition room, wasn't he?"

David wheeled round on him.

"Be your age, boy! You can't hold out after this. Don't you want the rotten case cleared up?"

"Yes, I do, now."

"Your painting says, as clearly as if it shouted the words aloud, that you found Burke in some narrow space. This figure might be toppling down a well. The whole thing is claustrophobic. For God's sake be sensible. Where was it?"

"Where Bert Lewis says he picked up the cigarette-case."

"Ah." David gave a long sigh of relief. "It dropped out of his pocket, I take it? When he was moved. Did you move him?"

"Yes."

Tom's face began to clear. As he told his story, relief in confession hurried his words. David had to stop him now and then. But the tale made sense: he was prepared to believe it was true.

Tom had gone down to the men's lavatory shortly after completing his drawings in the hall. He knew it was nearly closing time in the Gallery. He had gone down the usual way, but afterwards, afraid he might be locked in by mistake, he had taken a more direct route, up another flight of stairs and along a corridor closed to the public, because it led past the room that was being renovated. This passage was not actually closed, Tom explained. At the basement end, as in the hall, there was merely a wooden trestle with a 'No Admittance' sign on it. Anyone could get past the trestle.

"And you found Burke, dead, in this passage?"

"Yes."

"You did not kill him?"

"No."

"Yet you have painted him falling. Did you see him fall?"

"Must you be a hundred per cent literal?" Tom burst out, furiously.

"You used to be."

"I'm not, now."

"Splendid," said David. He went on, "I believe you, Tom. You wouldn't have let the cat out of the bag like this if you'd killed him. I suppose you've done it as a kind of justification for moving him. And that was to cover up for Chris Felton, wasn't it?"

"At the time, yes."

"But you don't think now that Chris did it?"

"I'm positive he didn't."

"Then who did? It leaves us with Lampton, and the Tufnell woman, doesn't it?"

"I suppose so. Would a woman be able to kill him the way it was done?"

"If the attack was sudden and unexpected, and a weapon was used. None was found, but, as we have said before, it would not have to be large, and there was plenty of building material lying about. The river was handy for disposing of it afterwards."

Tom nodded. Clearly, his thoughts were still for his friend.

"Whoever it was, tried to push it on Chris," he said. "Even after Lewis was arrested. That fire in the studio, those drawings of mine torn out."

"You told me you suspected Lampton of that."

"Or of putting Chris up to it. Perhaps to making the fire, too."

"Why?"

"He may have been told he would be suspected. Told he could protect himself that way."

"Possible, I suppose. So it's Lampton, is it?"

"I don't know. Mrs. Tufnell's face in the drawings seems to have been the objective for the after events. Only she was left in the book after all, wasn't she? Very confusing."

"I agree."

"Lampton tried to kill Chris," said Tom, firmly. "I'm convinced of that. Chris swears he did not attempt suicide. Says he had no reason to."

"What did he say, exactly? Can you remember the words he used?"

"Just those. He had no reason to commit suicide. I took it to mean he was satisfied by then that he wouldn't be suspected, since Lewis's trial was due soon. Everyone thinks he'll be convicted, after the evidence in the magistrate's court."

"It was meant to look like suicide, then. One of us will have to have a go at Chris. Get out of him what he knows that might be a danger to the real murderer. Perhaps the source of the drugs, too. An unqualified man must have an illegal source. Lampton knew things were getting out into the open. I'd like to talk to Lampton, too."

"You trust *me*, then?" said Tom, with a sidelong look at David.

"I do. I can't guarantee Mitchell, though. And that's who is going to hear your story now, my lad. Come downstairs while I get him on the 'phone."

Shortly afterwards Tom and David left the house together. They were talking as they went up the road, preoccupied with the immediate problem of Tom's too long withheld evidence. So they did not notice Mrs. Tufnell on the pavement opposite.

Chief-Superintendent Mitchell was used to people coming forward with fresh evidence long after a criminal event. It was usually dictated by their own needs, not his. But he thought it was particularly maddening that this youth should turn up sponsored by David Wintringham. He adopted a specially severe manner in dealing with him. Tom had enough good sense to submit to this quietly. In his own mind he realized now what a fool he had been from the start.

"I suppose you made sure he was dead, before you took it

on yourself to cart him off, and hide him?" asked Mitchell, witheringly.

"He was quite dead. There was a door into the big room a few yards from where he was lying. I carried him inside, and put him down under some sacking."

"Having jumped to the conclusion that your friend had killed him?"

"Yes."

"Why did you suspect Felton rather than Lampton? You liked the one, and disliked the other, didn't you?"

"I knew Chris had an outsize grudge against Burke. I did not know at that time that Lampton knew him, even."

"But you know, now?"

David intervened.

"I told him only to-day," he said.

Mitchell turned back to Tom.

"It may interest you to know that Felton was seen at a pub in Westminster, by himself, half an hour before the time you say you found Burke. That doesn't prove he didn't kill him. It does show you told us a pack of lies the first time."

"You know that, anyhow," said Tom.

"It doesn't encourage us to place much reliance on your word. We didn't find any traces of his being moved."

"I was wearing gloves, if that is to the point."

David spoke again.

"Burke has never been supposed to have been killed at the exact spot where he was found, has he?" he asked. "He was hidden there, but it never has been suggested that he was standing among all the building stuff when he was struck down."

Mitchell ignored this interruption.

"How did you leave the Gallery, Drummond?" he asked. "By the hall door?"

"No. I didn't dare. By that time I knew I was late. After closing time. It would have attracted too much attention to get someone to let me out. Besides, I was in a cold sweat thinking Burke might have already been seen by someone who had rushed off to get help. I didn't think of that when I moved him. I didn't hear any noise, but those damned passages are as silent as hell. So I went back round them. I found a side door. It was unlocked."

"Bert Lewis," said Mitchell, bitterly. "Had his escape route all ready. Well," he went on, "I don't know that this gets us very much further, and it doesn't knock down the case for the Crown as much as you two seem to think."

"It supports Bert's story of finding the cigarette-case without the body. If the case fell out of Burke's pocket, as I think it did."

"What about the wallet?" asked Mitchell. "Did that fall out, too?"

"You haven't proved Lewis had it, or the money in it."

"Perhaps you took it?" Mitchell said, looking at Tom.

"I did not."

"All right. Would you like to tell me the real reason why you've decided to bring me this story now? Apart from Dr. Wintringham's high faluting stuff about some painting you've done?"

"Yes. I'll tell you. I think someone wants to kill Chris. I think he's in danger. Now he is cured of his addiction, I think he is a danger to whoever it was killed Burke."

"What is the connection between the addiction and Burke?"

"He knew," said Tom. "Chris told me he knew. Burke ticked him off for doping, once. Chris had no idea how he knew about it, and it made him hopping mad."

"Felton never told you where he got his drug?"

"No. I asked him if it was Lampton, but he wouldn't say. He got upset when I asked him. Said his mother was involved."

"His *mother*!" said Mitchell, with a curious emphasis.

"Mrs. Felton is a pretty close friend of Lampton's," said David.

The Superintendent looked as if he would speak, but changed his mind.

"Very well," he said. "That's all I want from you at present, Drummond. I'll call you if necessary. You won't be leaving Dr. Wintringham's house, I take it?"

"Not at present," David answered for him.

As they left the Yard, Tom muttered his thanks.

"What we need," said David, "is a drink. Now I wonder which of the pubs in Westminster was patronized by Chris Felton that night? Would you have any sort of clue?"

Tom knew of two that he and Chris had visited in the past, and where they were known.

"Then we might have two drinks," said David. "One at each—if necessary. I should like to know if anyone met Chris that evening after he left the Gallery. I think he may have been waiting for someone, and Mitchell knows, but did not tell us."

"Who? Lampton?"

"Actually, no. I think perhaps his real mother, Mrs. Tufnell!"

After David had taken Tom away to Scotland Yard, Jill decided to do something herself. She could not bear to sit at home all the evening, chasing her thoughts round and round, and arriving nowhere. She made up her mind to see Chris Felton, or, if he were not at home, his mother. Mrs. Felton might be able to help her to make up her mind about Tom. And whether she could bear to have him living in her house any longer.

Hurrying away, with the sight of Tom's picture burning her memory, she too failed to notice Mrs. Tufnell, standing with her hand up near her face, behind the pillar box, as if posting a letter.

But Pauline, who had repented of her childish breakdown long before she reached her own room in Highgate, and had hastened back to assure Tom of her continued love and trust, did see the dowdy figure still moving slowly up and down near the Wintringhams' house. She hurried inside, when Nanny opened the door, hoping to avoid having to speak to the queer creature again.

Mrs. Tufnell made no attempt to stop her. She waited for ten minutes, then crossed the road, went up to the Wintringhams' front door, and rang the bell.

Chapter XVI

MRS. FELTON'S flat was very much as Jill expected it to
be, except for the photographs.

It was a service flat in that part of St. John's Wood nearest
to Regent's Park. It was compact and neat and self-con-
tained, having a hall inside the front door, from which the
three rooms opened. There were six of these flats on each
of the five floors of the building. This was arranged on three
sides of a square, with communal and well-kept gardens at
the centre. The parts were marked East, West and
South. Mrs. Felton lived on the second floor, South.

Having asked her way at the porter's desk inside the main
doors, Jill took herself up in the lift. Mrs. Felton was in,
surprised to see her, but remembering their conversation at
the hospital, quite ready to be welcoming.

"How nice of you to call, Mrs. Wintringham! I've just
come home from an afternoon at the pictures."

"Have I come at an awkward time?" Jill asked. Mrs.
Felton was wearing the spangled turquoise hat she remembered from her first encounter with her. But she still looked
anxious and harassed, and her eyelids were swollen with
recent crying.

"No. No, of course not. Can I get you a glass of
sherry?"

When Jill refused, the other said, almost with passion,
"You must! I mean, I badly want a drink myself." She
gave an artificial laugh, aware of the strangeness of her
manner, and trying desperately to cover it. "Please have a
drink with me," she went on, giving up all artifice.

"All right," said Jill, and added gently, "I'm so sorry."

Mrs. Felton went away and came back with a tray, on
which were two glasses of dark golden sherry, already poured

out. Jill, who disliked sweet sherry, took one, concealing her disappointment. Mrs. Felton began to sip hers, greedily.

As the conversation had lapsed, Jill looked at her surroundings, leaving it to her hostess to start a fresh topic. The furniture, she saw, was dull, but reasonably good. Perhaps it was a furnished flat, she thought. There was a good deal of shiny mahogany, and a few ornate pieces of rosewood from the Edwardian days of its popularity. The ornaments were in very poor taste, and as gaudy as Mrs. Felton's glittering hat. But the photographs, as she had noticed before, were unexpected. They consisted mainly of groups of uniformed girls, with a few white-coated men sitting in the middle of the front row.

"Was your husband a doctor?" she asked, and then wondered if she had dropped a specially heavy brick. She remembered that she did not know for certain if Mr. Felton was alive or dead. But certainly the groups were of doctors and nurses.

Mrs. Felton showed no signs of added strain.

"No," she said, "he wasn't a doctor." Then she added, surprisingly, "He was a patient."

"A *patient*?"

"Of mine," Mrs. Felton said simply. "I was a nurse."

"Oh, I see."

Any idea that Oswald Burke's sister, Mrs. Tufnell, might be disguised under the name of Felton, faded from Jill's mind. She saw that her plump hostess was watching her closely.

"I think it is only fair to tell you why I have come here," Jill said. "It was not so much to see you, as your son."

Mrs. Felton's face grew paler. She put down her empty glass with an unsteady hand.

"He is not my son," she said, slowly.

So that was it, Jill thought. The obvious alternative.

"My husband and I have been thinking that might be the case. He is Mrs. Tufnell's son, isn't he?"

"Yes." The word was a sob, and Mrs. Felton turned away, fumbling for her handkerchief.

"Will you tell me?" Jill asked, gently. "It is important, you know."

"Of course it's important. I've had the police here, asking for her. She's on the rampage again, and then Chris——"

"Tell me from the beginning. From when Chris was a little boy."

It all came pouring out now, and Jill listened, filled with pity for this woman's many frustrations and disappointments.

She had gone to nurse Christopher Tufnell when he was six, at the time of his first abdominal attack. He had always been a nervy little boy, and very spoiled, and he had become very much worse during the fortnight he had been in hospital, having his condition investigated. The children's specialist in charge had recommended conservative treatment at home, with a nurse trained in children's diseases. The boy's former nanny, a lazy and indulgent woman, had been sent away, and Nurse Cooper, as she was then, installed in her place. For the next six years she had looked after him. His father was a difficult, morose man, unhappy in his marriage and helpless where his strange wife was concerned. He hardly ever wanted to see the boy, who had turned out so different in every way from the sturdy little son to whose companionship he had looked forward. The mother, whom the small boy worshipped with a strange passion, was particularly bad for him. Most of the time she was wrapped up in her day-dreams or following the call of her brief wild infatuations for various men of her acquaintance. But sometimes, usually when one of her fantasies had been exploded, she would seek out and monopolize the boy, spending all her time in the nursery, invading his strictly kept meal and rest times, and taking him out on long exhausting expeditions, from which he came back too tired almost to move.

The result was always the same. Pain in the tummy, loss of appetite, lassitude, rise of temperature. The doctor would be called, at Tillingham, Dr. Redford, and the boy would be in bed for weeks. Meanwhile Mrs. Tufnell would have developed a new attraction, a fresh passion.

Mrs. Felton spoke bitterly, and Jill did not blame her.

"After the divorce, Chris was in his mother's care?" she asked.

"Yes. She sent me away. I was broken-hearted. It was a disgraceful thing, letting her have him. I went back to general nursing, which was easy enough to find. Private nurses were getting very scarce by then, as I expect you know."

Jill nodded.

"That was when I met Mr. Felton. I nursed him through a slight heart attack, and—well, we got on together very well —so after he was better, he took to asking me out, and then we were married." Mrs. Felton paused, seeming to look back over her brief years of married comfort. "He was very good to me," she said. "He was well off. I'd never lived so well before. But he died two years later. His heart again. We had no children."

Jill understood the depth of feeling in this last quiet confession. Nurse Cooper must have married in the hope of children, of having a baby of her own to replace the little boy to whom she had devoted six years of her life, and whom she had lost with such cruel finality.

"And it was just after his death I heard from Mr. Burke," she said.

"About Chris?"

"Yes. His mother had broken down completely and was in hospital. His own wife was not strong enough to have the boy living with them."

"That's a lie," thought Jill, who had heard David's account of Mrs. Burke.

"Mr. Burke wanted me to have him back. For the holidays and that. He was at a boarding school. A special one, small, for delicate boys. His uncle was going to move him to another school, where his mother was not known, and where the life was more normal. Christopher seemed pleased with the idea of coming back to me. We'd always been good pals. And he'd been badly scared when his mother began to go round the bend. It was in the holidays. She had begun to wander about, talking to herself, and once or twice threatened suicide."

"It must have been a ghastly experience for a boy of fourteen," said Jill, warmly.

"It certainly was. At first he said he only wanted to get away from her, and forget her altogether. He wasn't going to be tied to a mental mother; all that sort of thing. He took to calling me mother, then he had it out with his uncle, and insisted on changing his name to Felton for his new school. Not legally, he was too young, you understand. How I wished my poor husband was alive. He'd have done Chris a world of good. I don't feel I've made much real difference to him since I've had him back. That was why I let him go to Hugh—Mr. Lampton. But it seems to have been a failure, too. Drugs. Chris swears Hugh didn't give them to him, but I have my suspicions. So had Mr. Burke."

"I see. Was that part of the reason why Chris hated his uncle?"

Mrs. Felton nodded her head vigorously.

"Yes, it was. It was all mixed up with him wanting to be an artist, too. I had to encourage him, you see. If you don't let him have his head, up to a point, he gets really ill. You can't have that sort of thing established in a child, and expect to eradicate it, entirely. The same pattern crops up, later on. The doctors all say so."

Jill agreed that it was a most difficult case. Privately she took back all the hard thoughts she had entertained about Mrs. Felton. She had done her best, a most persistent best, to the very limit of her capacity. No one could do more than that.

"It was really Chris I came to see to-day," she said. And she told Mrs. Felton about Tom's picture and confession.

"So you see how very important it is to find out from Chris all he knows about where Tom was, and Lampton, and his mother, on that afternoon at the Westminster Gallery. When, exactly, he was with each of them, and for how long. Whether any of them spoke to Mr. Burke, and when and where. This new light Tom has given us on the case still doesn't tell us who struck the blow that killed Mr. Burke. I feel sure it was not Tom, but I can't prove it."

"It wasn't Chris," said Mrs. Felton, quickly.

"But you can't prove that, either."

"No, I can't."

"When can I see him?" Jill asked. "Is he at home, now?"

Mrs. Felton turned a ravaged face to her.

"He's not been here since the day before yesterday," she said. "His mother came here to see him, and they went out together. He never came back."

"You mean—— You mean——?"

"She's got her hooks into him again. After all these years. After all I've tried to do——"

Mrs. Felton could not speak for her tears, and Jill found that she could not be comforted. But she was profoundly uneasy. Was Chris's absence really of his own choosing?

"Mrs. Felton," she said, urgently. "I don't believe Chris would leave you like that, without a word, after all you have done for him. Oh, I know he seems to have no principles or consideration for people, or manners, even, but that was when he was doping. Tom is sure he is cured, at any rate temporarily. I think we ought to find him."

Mrs. Felton blew her nose, but said nothing.

"Where is Mrs. Tufnell living?" Jill asked.

"I don't know. She left the place where she's been ever since she came out of hospital. She must be somewhere in London. I've tried the only address I know that she might have gone to."

She looked helplessly at Jill, but made no objection when the latter took up the telephone receiver and got on to Scotland Yard. When she had finished she said, "Steve Mitchell has been following Mrs. Tufnell's movements. They saw her with Chris the day before yesterday, but lost them. However, they traced Mrs. Tufnell back last night to a house in Acton. Nineteen, Acacia Road."

"But—but——" stammered Mrs. Felton, thoroughly roused. "I went there yesterday, myself. It's the address I thought of. Where Hugh's friend stays when she's in London. Phyllis Marks. She's never looked at another man since she met Hugh in Tillingham all those years ago. She's a friend of mine, too."

"Then why didn't you ask her——? "

"She wasn't there. The house was shut up. It's for sale. There's a board out. It gave me such a shock."

"I wonder if the Yard know that? " said Jill.

"Ring them again and tell them."

Before she had time to pick up the receiver again, the bell rang.

"Go ahead," said Mrs. Felton.

The call was brief.

"Who was it? " Mrs. Felton asked. "Wrong number? "

"By no means. It was Mr. Lampton. He wanted you, or Chris. I said you were both out."

"I heard you. Why——? "

"You must come with me," said Jill, firmly. "I said you were out, and you must be out. Get ready while I ring the Yard again."

"Where are we going? "

"My home. Hampstead."

Mrs. Felton, subdued and obedient, went with her.

Pauline was not altogether surprised to find the studio empty when she went upstairs. The whole house seemed empty. Nanny, when she opened the door to her, said briefly, "They're all out, miss. Mrs. Wintringham and all. You'd best wait up there, though. They'll be back before long, I shouldn't wonder."

When she reached Tom's room, Pauline sank down in a chair, exhausted. She had hurried away, and then she had hurried back. A pointless exercise, she reflected bitterly.

She sprang up again and went to the two easels, both covered now. She lifted the cloths in turn. Symington-

Cole's stern, self-assured, ascetic face seemed more than ever a lifeless artifact. The other, the product of Tom's dreadful experience, no longer unnerved her. She began to see the beauty of the pattern, the richness of sombre colour; like a church in Lent, she thought suddenly, and was amazed at herself. She had not been inside a church for years, in Lent, or at any other time. Except for a friend's wedding, two years ago, when she had been a bridesmaid.

She followed up her thought. The picture had some affinity with medieval primitives, she decided. In modern terms it was a sort of descent from the Cross, without the piety, or the doctrine of hope, without the reverent faithful sorrowing friends, with only the pain and the despair and the apparent failure.

"Who's being blasphemous now?" she asked herself, and heard the door open behind her.

Turning quickly, thinking it was Tom, and ready to throw herself into his arms to ask forgiveness for her wicked suspicions, she checked violently, nearly tripping herself.

She saw the woman who had spoken to her in the road. Persistent old faggot, she thought.

"You can't see Dr. Wintringham," she said, loudly. "He's out and Mrs. Wintringham, too. I wonder Nanny—I mean the housekeeper—didn't tell you when she let you in."

"I didn't ask her." The woman spoke in a quiet educated voice, and Pauline was checked by it. "I asked for Tom Drummond. She said his room was at the top of the house, but he might be out still. She said I should find you here."

"Why do you want to see Tom? Why on earth?"

Pauline's earlier conclusions about this woman came crashing down. She began to feel frightened. The stranger was moving about the room, picking up things and putting them down. Her eyes were wide and vacant as she did this.

"Who are you?" asked the girl.

"I am Oswald Burke's sister," Mrs. Tufnell told her. "My name is Tufnell. I am Christopher's mother."

"Chris *Felton*?"

"That is not his real name. He is my son. Tom Drummond tried to kill him, but he failed. He tried to drive him to suicide. He killed his uncle, my brother, and tried to make them believe my son was guilty. He wants Chris to die, because he is jealous of his art."

"That is all nonsense," cried Pauline. "It's a pack of idiotic lies, and you know that as well as I do. If you don't know it, you must be mad."

Mrs. Tufnell, moving with astonishing speed, was upon her before she could defend herself. Her right arm was twisted back and she heard the forearm bone snap. Sick with pain, she fell on to Tom's camp bed, and lay there, shivering and moaning, expecting some final blow to fall. When none did, she forced herself to look up. Mrs. Tufnell was standing over her, with Tom's penknife in her hand.

"If you move, I shall kill you," Mrs. Tufnell said, in a quiet, matter-of-fact voice. "It is not you I really want to kill. It is Tom Drummond, for what he has done to Chris."

Pauline could not move. Her broken arm prevented that in any case. But her fear paralysed her. She had no doubt that Mrs. Tufnell was insane, and that she had killed her brother. Her only hope lay in Tom's return. How long would that be?

Pauline's ordeal lasted nearly an hour. Several times the pain in her arm and the shock of the fracture made her nearly faint. Each time, when her vision cleared, there was Mrs. Tufnell, penknife in hand, standing over her, watchful, malignant.

Then there were steps on the stairs and voices coming nearer. Mrs. Tufnell gave a long sigh, and leaned nearer to Pauline.

"At last," she said. "Now is the moment. If you warn him when he reaches the door, I will drive the knife into your throat." She whispered these words with deadly ferocity, and stretched out a hand to bare the girl's neck for the deed. Pauline was too frightened to move her sound hand in her own defence. Maimed as she was, she would have no chance against the other's mad strength. But when she felt Mrs. Tufnell's hard fingers on her neck, she nearly screamed aloud.

The woman lifted her head, listening.

"He is not alone," she said. She tiptoed away from Pauline to the door, turning her ear against it. "I shall have to strike as he comes in. Nothing matters afterwards."

She pressed herself to the wall beside the door.

"He will not see me as he comes in. Neither of them will see me."

Noticing a gleam of hope in Pauline's face at these words, she said, threateningly, "If you warn them I will kill you, first."

"I won't warn them," Pauline said. She began to speak as loudly as she could, without shouting. "Mrs. Tufnell, I promise I won't warn them."

"Be quiet."

"But they'll see you, Mrs. Tufnell. Why don't you hide behind the cupboard, Mrs. Tufnell? The side near the window. No one can see you from the door, then. It will make it easier, *Mrs. Tufnell*!"

She was very nearly shouting, but she had impressed the mad woman with her crazy plan. She left the door to stand beside the big cupboard. From where she now was she could not see the door open. Pauline knew this. She nodded encouragement to Chris's mother, praying that her mood would not change again. The voices on the stairs had fallen silent: the footsteps also. Had they heard and were they creeping up silently, or had they gone away again, changing their minds about coming to the studio?

With enormous relief she saw the door begin to open, slowly.

"I think they have gone downstairs again, Mrs. Tufnell," she said, clearly. "But don't come from behind the cupboard until we are sure."

Tom, when he saw her lying on his bed, her twisted arm across her breast, her white face and staring eyes fixed upon him, strode forward into the room with a great cry of rage and grief. It was David Wintringham who struck the knife from Mrs. Tufnell's hand as she whirled to the attack.

It took the whole strength of the two men to subdue her. In the end she gave way, allowing them to seat her in a chair, where she sat moaning and rocking herself from side to side.

Tom turned away then to throw himself on his knees beside Pauline and gather her into his arms. She gave a little cry of relief and joy and fainted.

Chapter XVII

W H E N Superintendent Mitchell was put through to Jill his first feeling was one of exasperation. He had only just got rid of David and his protégé, Tom Drummond. Now here was Jill, with another upsetting, and seemingly unhelpful report. He sent for Sergeant Fraser.

" I thought you said Mrs. Tufnell went home last night to a house in Acton. Nineteen, Acacia Road? "

" That's right."

" I hear it is up for sale and deserted."

" It wasn't last night, sir. She went in and a light went on upstairs, and later it went out. They kept a watch in the road all night."

" Find out when the house was put up for sale, and get on to the agent who put up the board. Find out when exactly that was put up. Mrs. Felton knows the woman who lived there, and went to inquire this morning. No answer, and this board near the gate."

" Very fishy, sir."

" Get someone round there at once. You go ahead and deal with the house agent. I'll be along as soon as I can."

Mitchell disposed of other business as quickly as possible and was driven out to Acton. He found two police cars, a private car and an ambulance at the door. Also Sergeant Fraser with a bewildered, resentful young man in tow.

" What's all this, Fraser? " the Superintendent asked, moving quickly through the small crowd of onlookers.

" The agent, sir," said Fraser, indicating that he had carried out his assignment.

" Keep him," said Mitchell. " What's all the commotion? "

"I don't know, sir. Only just got here. The 'For Sale' notice——"

"Keep it," said Mitchell, striding forward into the house.

Here he met a local detective-inspector, the local police doctor and two men in uniform.

"Evening, Simmonds," he said. "What have you got?"

"Body of a woman. Been dead at least twenty-four hours."

"A *woman*?"

"Owner of the house. Miss Phyllis Marks. Put the house up for sale day before yesterday. Looks like suicide."

"How?"

"Cut her throat."

"No one else here?"

"She lived alone."

Mitchell's face darkened.

"I didn't ask you for her history. I asked you if there was anyone else in the house."

"Not unless they're hiding. I haven't looked for that," said the inspector, stiffly. "Following the report of these chaps," he indicated the two patrol men, "I came right away, and found the body. Isn't it what you expected?" he asked, with genuine curiosity.

"It is and it isn't," said Mitchell, briefly, and added, "Search the house."

The police doctor intervened. "I've other work to do if I'm not wanted," he began, but Mitchell rounded on him.

"With any luck we'll give you a fresh job here," he said. "Stick with me, please, doctor."

It was not a large house, and they had soon finished with it. Mitchell strode out into the garden. There was a pocket handkerchief of a lawn, a small toolshed and a lumpy rockery.

"Air-raid shelter," said Mitchell. "That's the ticket."

They found Christopher Felton at the back of the shelter. He was tied up and gagged and half mad with fear, but when they had brought him out, and the doctor had worked on him, he began to pull himself together.

"I went with my mother the day before yesterday," he

explained, "because she said she knew that Tom had killed my uncle. I was to help her to get him convicted, she said. I didn't like her manner, but I thought I ought to humour her. And when she told me we were coming here, to Miss Marks, I thought everything would be all right. Because I'd known Phyllis Marks for years. She was a friend of my—of Mrs. Felton's."

"Was?" said Mitchell, slowly.

The boy covered his face with his hands. When he looked up again he struggled to speak before any words came. "Yes, was. You must have found her."

"Go on."

"We got back here and my mother let us in with a key and said, quite casually, 'The house is going to be sold.' I said, 'Why?' and she said, 'Phyllis doesn't want it any more.' I began to be worried, because Phyllis hadn't come out to see us when we went in. Then mother took me upstairs and opened the bedroom door and said, in her vague, soft voice, the one she uses when she isn't normal, 'You see, she's dead.' I was sick, and then I felt awful. And then I forced myself to go in, and look at Phyllis. Her throat was cut, and there was blood everywhere. But on the table near her bed there was a hypodermic syringe and some ampoules and some pills. I gathered up the lot and took them down and put them in the kitchen stove. Then I wondered if she had any more of the stuff hidden away, so I had a good look through her cupboards and drawers. I found quite a bit more and destroyed it all."

"Was this the source of your own supply?" asked Mitchell.

"Yes. No. I don't know. I'll never tell you. I've stopped taking it. That's good enough, isn't it?"

"We'll discuss that, later. What happened next?"

"I'm sure my mother killed Phyllis. She said, 'Tom has been here. He's killed her. He wants to kill you. I'm going to hide you from him. I must.' I felt I had to go on humouring her, so I followed her out into the garden."

"Why didn't you break away, then, and get help?" Mitchell's voice was stern.

"You don't know my mother. For years I did every single thing she wanted. I had to. I thought her so wonderful."

"I know the story. I've had it all explained to me."

Mitchell did not add that what the story meant to him was chiefly the way it showed up Christopher's own eccentric instability. No use expecting him to behave like a normal, rational young man.

"So you went out together to the old air-raid shelter?"

"Yes. It was dark in the garden and quite black in the shelter. I could hear her breathing beside me, but I couldn't see a thing. I said we'd better have a torch or something, and directly I'd said it I was hit on the head and went out like a light. When I woke up I was tied and gagged. I didn't know if she'd gone or if she was still there. When you came in I thought it was mother and I'd had it."

He covered his face with his hands again, shaking all over.

"You're quite safe, now," said Mitchell. "Can he come with us, doc?"

"He'll do," said the doctor. He felt Christopher's pulse once more, patted his shoulder, and hurried away.

"No, don't get up," said Mitchell, kindly. "I'll leave you here for a bit. Brew him a cuppa," he said, turning to the patrol. "We could all do with one before we leave. I'll be back."

He went out of the room, first to direct the further investigations into the manner of Miss Marks's death, and then to interview the highly shocked estate agent's clerk, and finally to get the local police to cordon off the road, and dispose of sightseers. When it was once more in its normal, deserted, respectable evening condition, Mitchell and Fraser, with Chris Felton between them, set off in the remaining police car.

"Where are we going?" Chris asked, presently.

"Scotland Yard. I want you to make a statement, and then we shall have to consider where to put you up for the night."

" Are you going to arrest me? "

There was panic in the strained voice.

"Why should I? What for? Your story sounded authentic to me. We found the buckled remains of the hypodermic where you said you'd put it, in the kitchen stove. And the burst glass of the ampoule. Lucky you destroyed it all. Lucky for you, I mean."

Chris knew what he meant.

"I was afraid she'd cut my throat," he said. "I kept thinking of that, not of the dope."

It was at this point that the first message came through over the car's radio. A delayed message. It had been discovered after Superintendent Mitchell left. It was from the housekeeper at Dr. Wintringham's Hampstead home. She reported that a woman of doubtful sanity, giving the name of Tufnell, had called to see Mr. Drummond. The housekeeper knew there was only the young lady, Miss Pauline Manners, in the house, and felt anxious.

Mitchell asked a few rapid questions. This message had come in very shortly before Mrs. Wintringham's. The two had got mixed. Or rather they were thought to be two aspects of the same matter.

"Thought! " exploded Mitchell. "Why do they try to think? They'd get on better if they never did any thinking at all."

He gave a rapid order, which Christopher did not hear, and the car bounded on towards the centre of London.

But not to Scotland Yard. They turned off into Kensington and stopped in front of Hugh Lampton's house. Telling the others to stay in the car, Mitchell got out and ran up the steps. When the receptionist told him that Mr. Lampton was in, he felt a great load lifted from him. A few minutes later he was shown into the psychiatrist's consulting room.

Mr. Lampton greeted him with the same calm self-assurance as before. He asked him to sit down, and when the Superintendent refused, remained standing himself.

M

"I'm afraid I have some very bad news for you," Mitchell said. "But perhaps you have heard it already?"

He watched the other, closely. Lampton looked puzzled, inquiring. Mitchell told him of the dreadful discovery at 19 Acacia Road.

The response was exactly what he ought to expect, correct in every detail. The shock, the horror, the grief, the concern about the dead woman's reputation, carefully placed before his own. Then the questions. How did Mitchell know? When was the discovery made? What theory was held of the cause?

"Either suicide," said Mitchell, quietly, "or murder. And the former the more likely."

"Why?"

"Because she put her house up for sale before she died. The arrangements were made over the telephone the day before yesterday. A board was put up yesterday. A friend of hers, who wanted to see her, saw the board, and went away, as she got no answer to her ring and knock."

"A friend?" There was, perhaps, a little breathlessness about the voice, now.

"Mrs. Felton. A friend of yours, too."

"An acquaintance. Through her son, a patient of mine. As you know."

"Mr. Lampton," said Mitchell, in a very official voice. "We cannot, at the moment, properly identify the dead woman. I'm afraid I must ask you to come with me to the house."

"In what capacity?"

Mitchell was revolted by the callous, cold-blooded question.

"Shall we say, as a doctor?" he snapped, and immediately regretted his indiscretion. He saw the answering flash in Lampton's eye, the swift calculation.

"I am not a qualified doctor," the psychiatrist said, quietly. But he went with Mitchell out of the house.

Sergeant Fraser was on the doorstep. He slipped a written message into Mitchell's hand. The police driver opened the rear door of the car. Lampton, his head half-turned to watch the Superintendent, stooped and got in. Christopher's voice, high and shaken with sobs, reached him.

"Oh, Hugh, my mother's gone mad again! She's killed Phyllis Marks. She was going to kill me! Oh, Hugh!"

The police officers were silent. The car speeded on, north again. Chris sobbed out his story and Lampton sat, in stony silence, listening to him. Only once he lifted his head to speak to Mitchell.

"This is not the way to Acton."

"We have a more important call to make now. Mrs. Tufnell has been found."

There was silence. Then Lampton's voice came again, dry and expressionless.

"Where? Not—not dead?"

"Oh, no," said Mitchell, cheerfully. "Far from it. At Dr. Wintringham's house, and very lively indeed, I'm told."

"She's mad," whimpered Chris. "A mad murderess, and my mother. What shall I do, Hugh? What can I do?"

"Be quiet," said Lampton, in such an icy voice that Christopher's complaint was frozen on his lips.

Mrs. Tufnell was in the studio with the doctor and another doctor and Mr. Drummond, Nanny told them. The young lady had been sent to hospital to have her poor arm put up in plaster.

Mitchell nodded. His radioed message had reported all these details.

"We'll go up," he said. Chris, the last to leave the car, shrank back.

"Not me!" he begged. "Don't ask me to see her again. I won't! I can't!"

"No," said Mitchell. "Much better not."

He detailed the police driver to look after Chris and then, himself going ahead, Lampton in the middle, and Fraser bringing up the rear, the three men went up to the studio.

Mrs. Tufnell was talking volubly to the professional psychiatrist David had called in. Tom stood awkwardly by the window. David turned towards the trio as they entered the room.

"Poor woman," said Lampton, calmly, watching Mrs. Tufnell, who continued to explain herself, not paying any attention to the fresh arrivals. "As Chris says, she is completely insane. Just as she was in the first attack."

"I had to cut her throat," Mrs. Tufnell was saying. "She would not wake up to speak to me."

"Ah," said Mitchell. He began to understand.

"You see I knew what she had been doing, bringing those drugs to London. She works in a chemist's shop at Tillingham. Ask Nurse Cooper. She knows her very well. She had them from *him* at one time. We all did. She made up the prescriptions, and she made them up short, and gave the extra stuff to him. It was quite easy. The prescription would be made out for sixty tablets, say, and she would give the patient forty, and keep twenty. People don't count their pills, not most of them. If they did, he told them he'd only written them up for forty."

"When you say *he*, do you mean the chemist at Tillingham?" Mitchell asked, breaking into the rapid flow of words.

Mrs. Tufnell ignored him completely.

"They all tried to take my boy away from me," she went on. "Nurse Cooper and—and *he*, too, and then that wicked man over there by the window. But I got him back. I've put him where no one will find him, and I was told to give him something to send him to sleep, but I couldn't find it."

Again Mitchell spoke.

"Was that the syringe on the table by Phyllis Marks's bed?" he asked.

This time Mrs. Tufnell looked round.

"Yes," she said. "I don't know what became of it."

Mitchell moved to one side, and Mrs. Tufnell saw the man standing behind him.

"Hugh!" she whispered. Her face went quite blank and she fell silent, clasping and unclasping her hands.

"Poor woman," said Lampton, steadily. "Can it be true that she killed Miss Marks? If so, she may have killed her brother."

"I doubt that," said Mitchell.

"Why?"

"Look on the table," said Mitchell. "Those are the contents of her bag that Dr. Wintringham has laid out for us. Do you see that wallet?"

"Yes."

"It has Burke's initials on it. Mrs. Tufnell," said Mitchell, "did your brother give you his wallet, or did you take it from him?"

"Take it!" said Mrs. Tufnell, in a very astonished voice. "No. He gave it to me. Poor Oswald. He was always good to me about money. I often needed it, and I never liked to ask him. But he knew and he liked to help me. It was at the Gallery. I was desperately short, so for once I did ask him. I spoke to him, and we had a little talk in a passage off the hall. He told me to take the wallet and keep the money in it, and give him back the wallet sometime. You see, I had forgotten to take my handbag with me. I am often forgetful. I went straight away to find Chris and tell him how kind his uncle was. He did not appreciate him. I looked for Chris up and down those passages. Then I saw that man, who had killed Oswald."

She pointed an accusing finger at Tom.

"You went away to find your son," said Mitchell, bringing back her attention. "Where did you find him? Do you remember?"

"At a public house. I forget."

"Did you speak to Mr. Lampton outside the Gallery?"

Her face went blank again, but she said, "No. I avoided him. He was avoiding me."

Lampton drew a long, slow breath.

"She is very sure that Drummond killed her brother," he said. "Perhaps in all this maze and confusion in her mind there is something she could tell us to confirm her belief."

"No."

It was David who spoke, moving quickly to an easel near the opposite wall.

"No," he repeated, throwing back the cloth that covered it. "But this is what happened. This is true, isn't it, Lampton?"

They all heard the cry, terror-stricken, animal, that broke from the psychiatrist's throat. Then he turned and rushed for the window.

But Tom was there to grapple with him. As the two men swayed together, and the others closed in, Lampton got his right hand free. They all saw it raised, the edge turned to strike at Tom's neck. But Mitchell gripped the wrist and held on until Fraser and Tom between them overpowered the criminal.

"Thanks for the demonstration," panted Mitchell. "We thought you used that technique on Burke. Now we know."

Chapter XVIII

JILL and Mrs. Felton, having stopped on their way to Hampstead to find a meal, did not arrive there until after Mr. Lampton's arrest. All the same the house was in a state of considerable confusion.

The final struggle with the psychiatrist had been too much for Mrs. Tufnell. After a period of wild hysteria, she had withdrawn herself completely from the world of reality. She would neither speak nor move. When Jill and Mrs. Felton reached the house they found that arrangements had been made to remove the sick woman to a mental hospital. They also found Christopher, in the willing, but not very helpful charge of Tom Drummond.

In these painful circumstances Mrs. Felton proved her worth. Putting away the young man, who at once clung to her, crying like a child, she insisted upon going upstairs to Mrs. Tufnell. The latter did not recognize her, but she submitted to the familiar handling of the trained nurse, and before long Mrs. Felton persuaded her to move downstairs from the studio to David's room, and even to take a warm drink, laced with an appropriate sedative. The consultant psychiatrist waited until an ambulance came for her, and then left. By degrees a certain calm was restored.

"Chris and I had better be getting along, now," said Mrs. Felton, coming back into the drawing-room.

Jill looked at David, but he only nodded agreement. Chris himself, sunk in an armchair, with his head turned away from them all, made no sign.

"You will come home, won't you, Chris?" Mrs. Felton pleaded anxiously.

He lifted his head and looked at them all in turn.

"I suppose so," he said, listlessly. "Anywhere. Nothing

matters now. Now that Hugh—now that I know Hugh
wanted me dead ! "

A fresh spasm of pain crossed his face. Jill was astonished.
His friend and guide was indeed a fallen idol, but he was also
a man in peril of his life. But Christopher's concern was
not for him : it was solely for himself. She was repelled by
the young man's complete egotism, but her admiration for
Mrs. Felton was kindled afresh.

"You flatter yourself," said David, coldly. "Lampton was
never gunning for you. He was out for Tom's blood, not
yours."

Tom nodded.

"It's a bit confusing," he said. "The fire and Chris's—
illness, and Miss Marks's death. I can see he may have
wanted to involve Mrs. Tufnell, but why me? And how
would it stick? "

"He was afraid of you," said David.

"Afraid of *me*? "

"Yes. On two counts, at least. Go back to the beginning.
Mrs. Felton, I'm afraid you had a fatal, though perfectly
innocent hand in the start of it all. When Chris joined the
Art School and you followed him to London you picked up
again your friendship with Miss Marks, didn't you? "

"Yes. I thought it would be a kindness. They knew
about her and Hugh in Tillingham. She was dropped by
some of her old friends there."

"Exactly. And from there we have Chris starting treatment with Lampton. And from there we have Oswald Burke
on the war path to get his nephew away from the man."

"Oh," said Jill. "And of course Mr. Burke knew too
much about Lampton's past."

"Quite. As I have thought from the beginning, Burke
must have decided to loosen Lampton's hold on Chris by
gentle blackmail. Being Burke, he probably made it
extremely offensive, and Lampton lost his temper."

"It wouldn't help matters their both having seen Mrs.
Tufnell at the Gallery," said Tom, sensibly.

"Indeed, no. She certainly spoke to her brother and got

the wallet from him. We can't be sure whether Lampton spoke to her or not. I think he did, and planted the idea of Tom's intrinsic wickedness. But I'm positive that was before the murder, and I think the killing was unpremeditated."

"Didn't he talk to her outside the Gallery, on the Embankment?" Jill asked.

"No. He said he had, but in fact she beetled off to join Chris at the pub, shortly after she finished talking to her brother. Tom and I got confirmation of that at the pub."

"She was still in the Gallery after the murder, though, because she spoke to Bert Lewis," Jill reminded him.

"Yes. The whole thing happened very quickly. I think she spoke to Burke and went off to find Chris, who had just left. Burke accosted Lampton directly after the conversation between brother and sister, they retired up that passage, officially supposed to be closed; they quarrelled, Lampton struck and killed, and feeling appalled at what he had done, rushed off to the lavatory, to think out his next move. Tom must have only just missed him as he came up the stairs into that passage. Tom moved the body, and left the Gallery by the side door. Bert Lewis went into that passage to wait, as he thought, in safety. But Mrs. Tufnell came along, still looking for Chris. Perhaps she thought he might have joined his uncle there. She was too intent on her purpose to take in what Lewis was saying or look at what he was holding."

"I expect she told him to take the cigarette-case to the porter," said Jill.

"Very likely. Anyway, she left the Gallery then, and joined Chris. About ten minutes after you'd left yourself, Felton, wasn't it?"

"About that," Chris answered. He was sitting up now, listening eagerly. "It was still a bit before closing time at the Gallery. I had begun to be worried, thinking she might have got herself locked in."

"Right. Lampton was seen by Cyril Ellis in the lav, and later, looking ill, on the Embankment. Who was he waiting for?"

"Not Chris or his mother," said Mrs. Felton.

"Me?" asked Tom.

"Yes. I think you. I think he had already planned to pin it on you, if he could. He had probably seen you making drawings in the hall of the Gallery. He hoped to make some excuse to keep you talking, or perhaps make an excuse to go back into the Gallery for something he had forgotten. Anything to have you there, *until the body was found.* He banked on the attendants using that closed passage. As they obviously would. It was the shortest way to the basement of the building."

"But I disappointed him," said Tom, quietly.

"You disappointed him. And two days later he knew something else. The body had been moved. I think he jumped to a very natural conclusion, which was that you moved it. A stranger, he'd think, would have reported the find."

"And then we put Steve on to Bert Lewis, and he was stymied again," said Jill.

"Tom was responsible there, too," David reminded them. "That first time I went to see Lampton, he was very cagey. Made no suggestions of his own, but agreed with all of mine. Preparing the way, I think, in case Bert Lewis was convicted of the murder."

"Preparing the way for what?" asked Chris.

"For your death, I'm afraid."

"But I thought you said——"

"Perhaps I should have said, for involving Tom in your death. He was to be shown as responsible. It was Lampton's only chance of taking attention away from Burke; I mean, the real danger for him lay in a true interpretation of the motive for Burke's murder. He knew the case against Lewis was shaky; he knew I was not satisfied. He knew if the police began going into Christopher's past history, and present habits—I mean the habits you still had at that time, Chris— he was sunk. He must have persuaded Mrs. Tufnell, poor soul, to light the fire in the studio, and later cut Phyllis Marks's throat, as she lay drugged in her bed. Chris's overdose he could manage himself. On each occasion he was far away. He has complete alibis."

There was a moment of silence.

"Do you really think Mrs. Tufnell was capable of carrying out orders?" Tom asked, doubtfully.

"It must have been Mrs. Tufnell."

"Why not Phyllis?" asked Mrs. Felton.

"And a bona fide suicide?"

"Mother *said* she'd killed her," Chris reminded them.

There was a pause in the conversation, and they all heard the front-door bell ring.

"Now I wonder who that can be?" said Jill.

Nanny opened the drawing-room door.

"Mrs. Redford, madam," she announced, formally.

The widow of Oswald Burke moved stiffly into the room.

David, seeing her stop short, disconcerted by so many faces, stepped forward.

"Mrs. Burke——" he said, quickly.

"Redford," she answered. "We were married a week ago. That is why I know what has happened here this evening. They rang me up and told me. Hugh wanted me to know. That is why I am here."

They had all risen, and stood without moving, for the chill of her cold voice reached their hearts, warning them of a greater evil than they had so far heard.

"I am on my way to Scotland Yard," she went on, looking at David, ignoring the others. "You were quite wrong, Dr. Wintringham. Hugh did not kill Oswald. I am going there to prove it. I killed my husband."

David looked at her. Now he understood why she had been so difficult, so puzzling, so unwilling to discuss the case with him.

"Have you come to tell me, first?" he asked, mildly. "I wonder why."

She gave a little cruel laugh.

"To take down your infernal conceit," she said. "I have known Hugh for some years. Oswald sent me to him to ask him not to treat his nephew, Christopher. That meeting brought us together, but Oswald did not suspect anything until quite recently."

"But Phyllis!" cried Mrs. Felton.

"The Marks woman? She was very, very faithful, poor dear, but as far as Hugh was concerned, a complete back number. Useful, of course, but a back number."

"You killed her, too," said Jill.

"Yes, I killed her."

"I should like to know," said David, "just how stupid I have been. The quarrel with Burke was over you, I suppose, not over Chris?"

"Yes. It was unfortunate that I went to the Gallery at all that day. I was staying away with friends, but we came up to town for the day, and while my friend kept a dressmaker's appointment, I went along to see Hugh. He had gone to the Gallery. I followed. I did not think of my husband being there. After all, the exhibition had been on for some time. But he saw me, and then insisted upon talking to Hugh. It was very unfortunate. They ought never to have met, and it was my fault they met then. After all the business with his sister and later Chris, of course Oswald was beside himself. I joined them in that passage. Oswald did not notice me, as I came up behind him. I was sickened by the things they were saying to each other. I went into that big room to get away from them, and I saw pieces of wood and iron lying about. I took up a short metal rod and went back. I hit Oswald on the side of the neck, to stop him talking. He fell and died at once. Hugh went one way; I went another. I stayed in the cloakroom until it was time for the Gallery to close. Then I had to leave. I walked out and crossed the road to the river and dropped the rod in it. It was not very long; it went into my handbag; there was no blood."

Tom said, slowly, "It wasn't me he was waiting for, David. It was—this woman."

Mrs. Redford stared at him, but he returned her gaze, and after a few seconds she turned her head away.

"That drawing!" cried Jill. "The one that was torn out. Was Mrs. Burke in it?"

"I don't remember at all," Tom answered.

But Chris nodded.

"I lied when I said I didn't tear it out. Hugh asked for it. Just like that. He didn't say why; I thought it was because we were both in it. Of course I noticed her face in the background. But I didn't think anything of it. Why should I? She was my aunt, and it was natural she should be there with my uncle."

He turned with childish violence to Mrs. Felton.

"I want to go!" he said, passionately. "Take me out of here, Mother. I can't stay in the same room with her! She has ruined Hugh! Take me away!"

Mrs. Felton put an arm round his shoulders and led him away.

"You would have let that boy suffer," said David. "Or Tom or Mrs. Tufnell. You have murdered, and burned, and murdered again. Was it you in the air-raid shelter when Mrs. Tufnell took Christopher in?"

"Yes."

"You would have killed Chris after his mother left if he had not destroyed the drugs?"

"Yes."

"And you have destroyed your present husband."

Her eyes shone with a fierce light.

"I am on my way to Scotland Yard to save him."

"From a charge of murder, perhaps. Not from his very real crimes. They will carry a heavy sentence. You should have confessed before."

For a moment her face sagged. Then she drew herself up.

"Hugh would not wish me to suffer alone," she said, and turned and went away out of the house.

Mrs. Redford was sadly disillusioned at her trial, when it became evident that her marriage was simply a move on Lampton's part to secure him from any evidence she might give about his drug trafficking. She was found guilty of murder with diminished responsibility and received a life sentence.

Hugh Lampton Redford did not escape. On a very different charge he was sentenced to ten years' imprisonment.

Bert Lewis found himself back in gaol for five years. Both he and his wife thought he had got away with it very lightly. Mrs. Lewis was made much of by those neighbours who had been most censorious before, and Gladys found no impediment to rapid progress in her training.

Mrs. Felton took Chris on a voyage to the West Indies. He spent the time in a deck-chair writing his memoirs up to the time of his cure. The result was a cross between de Quincey and a Victorian tract, but it was published serially in a newspaper, and he found it financially rewarding. So he began another serial written from his mother's point of view. It seemed to Mrs. Felton that the Oswald Burke case might keep her adopted son gainfully employed for a long time.

Tom and Pauline got married as soon as her arm mended. After some months Tom, to his great surprise, and on the merits of his Burke picture, was offered a travelling scholarship. It was the Oswald Burke scholarship, founded under a bequest made in the art critic's will. Tom was the first to enjoy it. He spent some of the money paying the debts he had incurred on his honeymoon, and then set off with Pauline, hitch-hiking to make up for this. Italy was their immediate destination.

The house at Hampstead settled down to its former quiet routine.

"And a good thing, too," Nanny said. "With the summer holidays coming along in six weeks from now."

Jill agreed. She was thankful it was all over, though she was still haunted by the thought of Mrs. Redford's future.

"Will they ever let her out?" she asked David, one evening.

"I doubt it. Two murders and another planned."

"She'll just get older and older, thinking she let herself in for it to save a man who didn't care two pins for her."

"That's about it."

"Lampton Redford would have been convicted, wouldn't he? If she hadn't spoken."

"I don't know. Steve tells me she left plenty of evidence of her presence at 19 Acacia Road. As well as Mrs. Tufnell. They'd have started looking for the owner of the strange finger-prints. Steve had one or two hints, too, from the house-keeper receptionist at Redford's place, that didn't quite fit Mrs. Felton or Mrs. Tufnell. Steve's persistent. He might have made out."

"But you came a cropper," said Jill.

"I did. Unforgivable, really. You remember Lampton's reaction in the studio when he saw Tom's picture?"

"I wasn't there. But you told me. Go on."

"Well, if he'd hit Burke himself, the body would have fallen away from him. He would not have seen the face. Only a slumped figure, face down. But Mrs. Burke hit him, and Lampton was facing him. What he saw was what Tom imagined, and painted. He reacted to that because *he was not the killer*. And one more thing. He was in the army in the war as a doctor, not a combatant. He never learned any commando stuff. That method of killing with the hand was never part of his war experience. When he lifted his hand to Tom, it was just coincidence. I don't believe he knew what he was doing."

"Easy enough to explain—afterwards," said Jill, com-placently. "You made one big bloomer, darling. And about time, too."